FIC   Roberts, Willo Davis
ROB

Nightmare

$13.95   21360

DATE		
SEP 2 4 1992	SEP 2 9 1994	
OCT 0 2 1992	TATZ	
OCT 2 3 1992		
OCT 2 3	OCT 1 9 1994	
	DEC 0 2 1994	
OCT 2 9 1992		
NOV 0 5 1992		
FEB 1 6 1993		
MAR 0 8 1993		
OCT 0 1 1993		
OCT 1 8 1993		

Nightmare

Nightmare

WILLO DAVIS ROBERTS

A *Jean Karl Book*

Atheneum

New York

Atheneum
Macmillan Publishing Company
866 Third Avenue, New York, NY 10022
Collier Macmillan Canada, Inc.
Printed in the United States of America
10 9 8 7 6 5 4 3

Library of Congress Cataloging-in-Publication Data
Roberts, Willo Davis.
Nightmare / Willo Davis Roberts. —1st ed.   p.   cm.
"A Jean Karl book."
Summary: When a falling body strikes Nick's car as he drives under
an overpass, the police call the man's death a suicide, but Nick
suspects murder and finds his life in danger when he tries to
investigate.
ISBN 0–689–31551–1
[1. Murder—Fiction. 2. Mystery and detective stories.] I. Title.
PZ7.R54465Ni   1989   [Fic]—dc20
89–7038   CIP   AC

Nightmare

1

Seconds before the windshield shattered into a crazed, opaque spider web pattern, Nick saw the terrified face that would remain forever imprinted on his mind: eyes wide and unseeing, mouth stretched in a grimace of horror. Nick didn't hear the scream, but he knew there had to be one.

He had no conscious recollection of slamming on the brake, but the skid marks were there on the pavement afterward, proof that he had stopped as fast as he could.

Not that it mattered. The man who had fallen from the overpass onto the hood of Nick's old, blue Pinto was already dead, his neck broken when he struck the car.

Nick knew that, yet he saw the face again, hurtling toward him beyond the glass, and once more he flinched from the impact and the spreading pattern of splintering glass.

Nick yelled hoarsely, choking on his own protest, and then at last he woke himself out of the dream, gasp-

1

ing, finding the reality of his own bedroom no refuge from the nightmare. Because it had really happened; his crumpled Pinto, towed to the back of Tony's Wrecking Yard, was proof of that.

Nick drew a shuddering breath, fighting the panic the dream had evoked. He was soaked with sweat. The sheets were damp as well, tangled around his bare torso, and the blanket and pillow had fallen to the floor.

"Nick? What's wrong?"

His mother padded across the hall to his doorway, and he swore inwardly. "It's OK, Mom. Just another nightmare."

"Oh, Nick. I'm sorry. Would you like me to fix you a cup of cocoa?"

He stifled a groan. That was her solution to these damned dreams, a cup of cocoa, as if he were six instead of seventeen and had dreamed he was being chased by bears. "No, Mom, I'm fine. Go back to bed."

She hesitated, a dim shape there in the doorway. "Well, if you're sure."

"I'm sure," Nick said, and was unable to refrain from speaking through his teeth.

She'd realized that he didn't want her there, and she was hurt. He was sorry about that, but he couldn't help it. He wished they'd just leave him alone.

Nick heard their voices in the room across the hall. "Another nightmare," Elaine Macklin said, and then her husband's deeper voice made a rumbling reply. She'd closed the door by then, and Nick couldn't make out Steve's words, but he could guess at them.

"When is the kid going to stop waking us up at night with his bad dreams? It happened three days ago. It's over. Now when's he going to forget it?"

2

Nightmare

Nick sat on the edge of his bed, still shaking the way he had at the scene of the accident, getting chilled in the night air but unable to make himself crawl back under the covers.

He tasted bile in his throat, and resentment of his stepfather rose with the foul taste. Didn't Steve think he'd stop the dreams if he knew how?

His eyes stung, and Nick moved savagely, picking up the covers and the pillow to throw them on the bed. It wouldn't be light for another hour, but he'd never be able to go back to sleep. He reached out and punched the button on his digital alarm so it wouldn't sound when he was no longer there to turn it off, and wake his mother and Steve. That would be one more thing to annoy his stepfather.

He groped for jeans and a T-shirt, then found a sweatshirt in the chilly room. He carried his athletic shoes downstairs before he put them on.

Usually he woke up starving—it had long been a family joke that Nick had trouble getting through an entire night without a snack—but his stomach remained in a hard, painful knot. He wasn't hungry now. And it seemed like a long, long time since there had been family jokes.

Since his dad had died.

Since Mickey had left home.

Since Mom had married Steve.

He made his way quietly through the dark, silent house. He knocked something off the kitchen table, recognizing it when he bent to pick it up. Steve's uniform cap. Steve was a sergeant on the San Sebastian police force.

Nick had actually met Steve before his mother had.

3

A couple of years ago he and Larry, his best friend, had been writing what they thought were unbearably funny slogans on the pavement in front of the junior high school when all of a sudden a black and white came around the corner, hardly making a sound. It wasn't until the blinking blue and red lights came on that they realized they were in trouble.

Larry swore and Nick just stood there as the officer got out of the car and came toward them. Sergeant Macklin was a tall, well-built man who moved quickly and easily. He stood looking at what they had written. Nick expected him to order them into the back of the squad car; he was already imagining what his dad was going to say when he was awakened at midnight by a call from the cops.

"Out kind of late, aren't you, fellas?" Sergeant Macklin asked.

"Uh . . . we're on our way home. From the basketball game," Nick said.

"Folks expecting you before midnight?"

Nick cleared his throat. "Well, we didn't have a curfew, exactly. Just . . . after the game." It sounded lame and stupid. He *felt* stupid, and the words that had seemed so clever when they wrote them on the paving with orange spray-paint now looked stupid, too.

"You can't leave this written on a city street," Sergeant Macklin said. "You'll have to scrub it off."

"Scrub it off?" Larry echoed, incredulous. "It's paint, man! How we going to get it off?"

"I guess that's your problem. Because if there's a trace of it left by the next time I come on duty—that's at four tomorrow afternoon—I'm going to have to charge you with malicious mischief. Either of you have a police record?"

"No!" both of them said at once, shocked.

"If you want to keep it that way, clean off that paint before I get a chance to see it again. I'll want your names and addresses. Then you can go on home for now, in case your parents are worrying about you. But you'd better hit it early in the morning, because it's going to take a while to get that paint cleaned up."

It wasn't nearly as much fun removing the paint as it had been putting it there. But Steve Macklin hadn't reported them to their folks, hadn't charged them with anything. Nick was glad about that, though he wouldn't have said he exactly *liked* the man.

Nick remembered that first meeting now as he let himself out the back door. Dillinger roused from his rug in the kitchen to go with him, and Nick didn't protest his company. Dillinger was his buddy. He was a three-year-old fox terrier, mostly white with a few black and brown spots, and bright, friendly eyes. Only the white showed now in the predawn.

The house next door, beyond the hedge, was as dark as his own. For once that dorky Daisy wasn't spying on him, Nick thought idly as he opened the rear gate and let himself out into the alley.

He didn't have any particular destination. He just needed to go somewhere no one would bother him. He needed to think, to figure out how he was going to get over the things that had happened to him in the past couple of weeks.

He wished Mickey were here. He and Mickey used to talk for hours, before Mickey left home. Nick and his brother were closer than many brothers. Larry had three of them and couldn't stand any of them. But Mickey was neat.

Mickey was in Texas. A long way from California. And Larry was asleep; if Nick tried to wake him up, he'd wake up someone else in the family, too, and they'd both be out of favor for a bit. Besides, Nick didn't really want to talk.

He'd tried not thinking about the bad things, and that hadn't worked. Maybe now it was time to let all the memories flood over him, wallow in them, even, and see if that worked.

He sure hoped something was going to work, because he thought he'd go crazy if things didn't get better pretty soon.

A month ago Nick had been riding fairly high. He had a steady girl, Lisa Shafer, who was one of the prettiest girls at San Sebastian High. His Pinto was old, but it was in pretty good shape for its age and it was cheap to operate. That was important, because his after-school job at Bob's Super Service paid only minimum wage. Nick was getting good grades and had already been enrolled at SSCC, the community college. If his dad hadn't died, he'd planned on UCLA, but there wasn't money for that now. His dad's final hospital bills had been astronomical, using up most of the life insurance money after the hospitalization insurance had been exhausted. Maybe, Mom said, they'd be able to swing it for his last two years, especially since Mickey had decided he wasn't going to go to college.

6

Nightmare

Nick felt a little guilty about Mickey, though his brother had assured him that he didn't *want* to go on to school. "I'm gonna work for a year or two, maybe go in the Navy. What's the point of studying when I don't even know what I want to study? You know *you* want to teach science of some kind, so go, kid. Learn." Mickey had flashed that wonderful grin that melted so much opposition. "When you get rich, you can loan me money."

"You don't get rich teaching science," Nick said wryly, but though he had accepted what his brother said, he still felt twinges of uncertainty about the matter.

A month ago Nick had even begun to accept the fact that his mother had remarried less than a year after Joe Corelli's death. Steve wasn't so bad; he just wasn't used to kids, except delinquent ones, Mom said. She told Steve with painful earnestness that her sons had always been good boys, never got into any serious trouble. And to Steve's credit, he apparently hadn't told her about the episode with the spray paint.

Maybe if he hadn't still missed his dad so much, Nick might have found it easier to accept a stepfather. Or if Steve had been more like Joe Corelli.

Joe had been the manager of a shoe store, a job that paid the bills but gave him only minimal satisfaction. Nick vividly remembered his dad saying, "Don't get locked into the kind of thing I did, son. Choose something you really love to do, and go for it. Even if it doesn't pay a lot, if it makes you a living and you enjoy it, do it."

"You could change jobs," Nick had suggested. "You don't have to sell shoes the rest of your life."

Joe laughed ruefully. "No, I'm too old to change jobs. And I don't hate this job, I just don't get excited about it. What I get excited about comes after working hours, with my family."

Those times, on weekends with his father, were the times Nick missed with an aching longing that was almost a physical pain. Joe was a man who loved the outdoors, the mountains, the water, the woods. When Mickey and Nick were little kids, he'd taken them camping in a tent and sleeping bags. The year Nick was twelve, they'd acquired a little thirteen-foot trailer they'd pulled behind Joe's pride and joy, a four-wheel drive Ford pickup.

Elaine Corelli wasn't as much interested in wilderness adventures as the boys were. Most of the time it was just Mickey and Nick and Joe who headed for the Pacific beaches—the rugged ones to the north, not the "tame" ones of Southern California—or the wonders of Yosemite or Sequoia National Parks. Twice there had been memorable excursions to Death Valley in the spring, when the desert was wonderfully in bloom and there were small creatures to be sought out so that Mickey could photograph them and the others could enjoy their antics.

Their favorite place had been in the High Sierra, above Sonora, where they camped in isolated splendor, soaking up fresh, clean air and the scent of sun-warmed pines. It still made Nick's eyes smart when he thought about it, and how he missed those excursions and his dad.

For years Joe Corelli had talked about trading in the little trailer—which had eventually been exchanged for a bigger one so that Elaine would be more comfortable joining them—and getting a motorhome. Mickey and Nick had gone with him to choose it with part of the money from Grandpa Corelli's estate: an extravagance, admittedly, but Joe had paid off their house and they didn't urgently need anything else, and Joe had wanted one for so long.

Now the trips were ended. The motorhome sat in the side yard, undriven since Joe's death. Steve had no interest in it; he wasn't into camping or traveling. In fact he'd been pressuring Elaine to sell the thing—"It's too valuable to sit there and depreciate"—and she'd agreed that it was only sensible to do so. She'd even written out an ad to put in the paper. It was one more thing Nick had to be resentful about: His dad had loved the motorhome and the things it had enabled them to do. Joe was gone, and soon everything he'd cared about would be gone as well. Even if selling the coach meant he could go to UCLA as planned, Nick didn't know if he wanted to let it go. It was just too much a part of his father.

Mickey had lasted two months into Elaine's remarriage. He and Steve were at odds over virtually everything from Mickey's habit of leaving ice cream dishes and apple cores around in odd places to the more basic questions of what Mickey was going to do with his life. His blithe "I haven't decided yet" didn't set well with a man who had known from the time he was six that he intended to be a cop.

Nick had felt something close to panic when Mickey told him he was pulling out. "I called Uncle Ben and he said I could come and stay with him. He always needs help on the ranch. It'll be a change of scenery, and I can always join the Navy from there, or go on to school, or whatever I decide to do."

"It's not going to be fun here without you," Nick said with feeling.

"Yeah. But your temperament is different from mine. Work at getting along with Steve, huh? He means well. And he's good for Mom."

They both remembered clearly how difficult everything had been for their mother during the weeks Joe Corelli lay in the hospital, and then even worse after his death. Joe had always taken care of the bills, the house and car repairs, the decisions regarding insurance and taxes and all the other matters every family deals with. Elaine was not only grief-stricken but bewildered and helpless. Even coping with shopping and keeping a checkbook were beyond her for a few months, and the boys had taken over those chores, along with cooking the food nobody wanted to eat and doing the laundry.

When Joe Corelli died, the house was paid for, and there was money enough for his final bills, but there was almost nothing left over from Joe's insurance. When Elaine finally pulled herself together, she took the first job that was offered, as a waitress in the OK Cafe. She hadn't worked since her marriage nearly twenty years earlier, and she wasn't trained for anything that would have paid better. Being a waitress brought in enough for their basic living expenses.

It was through her job that Elaine had met Steve Macklin. Most of the cops stopped there for coffee when they were going on or off shift, and also for lunch sometimes.

Elaine was lonely, and so was Steve. He'd been divorced several years earlier, had no children, and as he told her, it was hard for a cop to meet nice women. He thought Elaine was nice, and he asked her out.

Nick had been surprised that she'd dated so soon after Joe's death, but Mickey had said, "She needs somebody, Nick. Somebody besides us. She and Dad had a good marriage; she was used to a man who looked after her, comforted her, helped her. Maybe this Steve will be good for her."

He was, though both the boys were shocked when Elaine told them she and Steve were getting married. "We need each other," she said, somewhat piteously, and the boys had tried to accept that because they could see it was true.

Two months later, Mickey had packed his stuff and hopped a bus to Houston. Nick missed him intensely and tried to hold himself together in a household that no longer seemed like home but some alien territory where he wasn't really welcome.

And then, in one day, the rest of Nick's world had caved in when he lost his girlfriend and a stranger broke his neck falling onto the hood of Nick's car, all within a matter of hours.

Nick desperately needed his father, or Mickey, but they weren't there. There was only his mother, who was more like a frightened rabbit than a pillar of support, and Steve. Steve, who only compounded Nick's problems, rather than helping to solve them.

2

Nick had had no warning that Lisa was about to break up with him after six months of steady dating.

He'd gone over to her house when he'd gotten off work Friday evening. Only it was Mrs. Shafer, not Lisa, who answered the door. Usually Lisa's mother greeted him warmly. This time, her face turned pink as soon as she saw him, and her manner was distinctly uncomfortable.

"Oh, Nick. Was . . . was Lisa expecting you?"

Even then, idiot that he was, he hadn't immediately gotten the message. "No, we didn't have a date or anything, but I got off a little bit early and I thought maybe we'd have time to catch the second show if she wanted to go."

"Oh! Well, I supposed she'd talked to you. . . ."

Ordinarily she would have invited him in. He was beginning to feel uneasy, standing there on the front steps, without knowing quite what was wrong. "Isn't she here, then?" he asked, and a moment later heard Lisa's laughter. She wasn't alone; there was a deeper male laugh, too.

Mrs. Shafer had gone a mottled red. "I was certain she would have spoken to you. . . ."

Intelligence finally began to seep through at that point. "No," Nick said, sounding and feeling stiff without yet totally understanding why. "I haven't talked to her since school yesterday."

"And she didn't say . . ." Mrs. Shafer's voice was faint. "Well . . . Just a moment, Nick. I'll call her."

And she left him standing there on the porch in his coveralls from Bob's Super Service, feeling like a thumb that's just been hit with a hammer.

When Lisa finally showed up—Nick heard the whispered conversation even though he couldn't make out the words, and realized Lisa was resisting coming to the door—she had a defensive air.

"Oh, hi, Nick. I wasn't expecting you."

His heart had begun to pound, but he kept his voice cool. "I gathered that. Have other company, do you?"

"Yes, actually. You know Jim Packard, don't you?"

Nick's heart sank. All he wanted was to get away, and he wished he weren't wearing greasy coveralls, and he didn't want to hear anything about Jim Packard. He already knew more than he wanted to about Jim, who had played left end on the San Sebastian Wildcats last year and was now attending some prestigious college back east. He was probably home on spring break.

"Yeah, I know Jim." Nick held his ground, pride keeping him from fleeing like a little kid, even though suddenly a number of things were falling into place. "Are we still on for tomorrow night, or is Jim going to take care of that as well as tonight?"

Lisa ran her tongue over her lips as if they'd suddenly gone dry. By this time Nick had noticed that she was wearing a skirt and a sweater he'd never seen before, rather than jeans. He and Lisa had seldom gone anywhere they needed to dress up, so he guessed the clothes were a tribute to Jim Packard.

"I was going to call you," Lisa said, and now she sounded less assured. "Jim's going to be home for a couple of months—he hurt his knee and will have therapy here instead of in Boston."

"And you're going to be part of the therapy?" Nick couldn't help asking.

Lisa gave him a level look. "Jim and I were friends a long time ago, when he was a year ahead of us in school. We're still friends."

Nick swallowed hard. "Sure. Well, I guess that means we won't be seeing each other much for a while, then?"

Relief etched itself on her pretty face, and she pushed back blond bangs. "You don't mind, do you, Nick? I mean, Jim's alone—everybody he knows is away at college, except him."

"And you," Nick said. "Well, I'll see you around, then."

He never remembered going down the steps or driving home. It wasn't that he and Lisa had ever made serious plans for the future or anything like that. But they'd had fun together, and he'd liked having everybody at San Sebastian High refer to Lisa as "Nick's girl." He'd felt she understood his problems at home, and they'd been able to talk about almost anything, no matter how personal.

Except Jim Packard, it seemed. Had Lisa stayed in touch with him, by mail or phone, since Packard went off to school in the East?

She hadn't even had the decency to face him and tell him herself, but had left it to her mother to say that she had changed her interest to Packard. He'd never have treated her that way, Nick thought. It hurt. It hurt a lot.

He'd thought he meant more to her than this.

His mother was in the kitchen. "Oh, hi, honey. There's a letter for you, from Mickey." She indicated the envelope on the kitchen table. "And fresh oatmeal raisin cookies."

He wasn't hungry, but he tore open the letter from Texas. Mickey had a big, sprawling first-grade sort of handwriting, different from Nick's own small neat hand. Nick had read halfway through the letter before he realized the words weren't registering; he took a deep breath and started over again.

"Anything exciting happening in Houston?" his mom asked, and Nick shook his head.

"No. Just touching base with us, I guess. He likes working with cattle and horses, and Uncle Ben has a new Jeep. Mick's been driving it. It's getting warm, really springlike, he says."

He couldn't tell her the rest of it. Not the part about the girl Mickey had met, a pretty girl named Brenda, who lived on an adjoining ranch. Some of what Mickey wrote made Nick's ears burn, and would have been entertaining if he'd been in a mood to be amused.

The phone rang and his mother answered it, then handed it to Nick. "It's Larry." She waited hopefully for him to hand over Mickey's letter, but this time he couldn't. Nick folded it and stuck it in his pocket, trying not to see her disappointment as she left the room.

"Hi, Larry," he said into the phone.

His best buddy immediately picked up on his voice. "What's wrong, Nick?"

There was no waltzing around with Larry. "Lisa just dumped me. For Jim Packard."

"Aw, crap!" Larry said. "Listen, you OK?"

"Wonderful," Nick told him. "How about tying one on with me tonight? Pig out on pizza? My treat."

"Jeeze, Nick, I wish I could. My dad's got a load of produce to go to San Francisco, and the regular driver is sick so Dad's going to take it himself. He wants me to go with him. We're supposed to leave right after supper. That's what I was calling to tell you. I can't double-date with you tomorrow night. Oh. I guess you won't be going out anyway."

"You got it," Nick said, striving to sound as if it didn't matter, though he knew Larry would know better. "Have a good trip. I'll see you in school on Monday."

"Right, if we get back by then. I'm hoping he'll let me drive part of the way, so he can sleep. See you, buddy."

Nick replaced the phone and turned to see his mother standing in the doorway with an armload of clothes, freshly folded from the dryer.

"Nick? You've broken up with Lisa?" she asked, distressed.

"No big deal," he said, wishing she hadn't overheard any of that. As Mickey had once put it, Elaine Macklin tended to bleed over all their problems, even the little ones, and the boys tried to spare her that, especially after their father's death.

"I'm sorry," she told him, her blue eyes going misty.

"It's OK, Mom. I'm a big boy, remember? This is the kind of thing that Steve says happens to everybody."

That wasn't the right thing to say, either. "He means well, Nick. He just doesn't understand how things were with us, before. What a close family we were."

Nick wasn't hungry, but anything was better than continuing this unwelcome conversation. "I guess I'll have a few of those cookies and a glass of milk, if that's OK. What's for supper?"

She hugged the stack of towels against her breast. "Liver and onions," she said, with a note of apology.

Nick hated liver and onions. When his dad was alive and she made liver and onions, she'd allowed the boys to have hamburgers if they wanted them. Steve thought it was unreasonable that Elaine had to cook more than one meal, as he put it, and he insisted that everyone eat the same thing.

"Unless it's yogurt or Spanish rice," Mickey had once pointed out. "If *he* doesn't like it, that's different."

"I was going to meet Larry for pizza," he said, counting on his mother to have lost track of the telephone conversation after the mention of being dumped by Lisa. "I won't be out late, though."

He took the cookies and milk and went up to his room with Dillinger trailing behind him for his share of the snack. Why was he always being made to feel guilty about something? He knew it hurt his mother's feelings that he didn't talk to her in the way that he'd been used to doing, but how could he when he couldn't criticize

17

Steve, even though Steve was free to criticize him? Yet he knew it was important to her to be loyal to her new husband; she was always doing a balancing act between Nick and Steve.

"I feel sorry for Steve," Mickey had said once, laughing. "He doesn't really approve of our eating away from home—especially on a night we're having something you and I don't like—but he wants Mom to himself, so he lets us go."

He'd have trouble stopping me, Nick thought now, depositing the plate and glass on his nightstand and peeling off his coveralls before he flopped on the bed. God, I wonder if I can stand living in this house until I get through two years of junior college, if he keeps on treating me like I'm some stupid kid.

Dillinger nudged him firmly with a wet nose, and Nick fed him half a cookie and chewed the rest of it himself, lost in morose thought. Probably his mom would tell Steve about the breakup; would Steve comment on it to *him*? Nick didn't think he could stand it if his stepfather belittled the relationship, or Lisa. Not tonight, anyway.

He almost got out of the house later without any direct contact. But his timing was bad. He had bypassed the kitchen and was heading for the front door when Steve came out of the living room, newspaper in hand.

"Don't go anyplace, Nick. Dinner's going to be on the table in five minutes."

"I'm eating out," Nick said, and would have kept on going, but Steve's voice held him.

"I thought maybe you'd finish cleaning out the garage tonight, the way I asked you to do." Steve sounded neutral, but Nick always felt as if there was a steel edge to his stepfather's words, just under the surface.

"Not tonight," Nick said tightly. "I've made other plans. I'll catch it Sunday afternoon, OK?"

He was not reassured by the apparent mildness of the observation. "I asked you to do it a week and a half ago, if I remember right."

"Sure. I'll do it Sunday," Nick repeated, and was relieved when Steve didn't follow him out the door and down the front steps to insist. Nick knew he'd blow up for sure if that happened. What was the big deal about hurrying to clean out the garage, for gosh sake? Probably Steve just wanted his predecessor's belongings where they wouldn't be a reminder that Elaine had been married before, though that seemed dumb when they were living in the house that Joe Corelli had bought and paid for.

Nick's mood was black and bleak. He wished Larry wasn't off on a truck ride to San Francisco, or that he himself were going along. He'd done that a few times, and Larry's dad was a good sport to be with.

He was scarcely aware of where he was driving. It didn't matter, only that he was by himself, that he didn't have to listen to anyone's condolences over losing Lisa to a Harvard man, or whatever it was. Some of his pain was beginning to turn toward anger at Lisa, but he wasn't ready to hear anyone else express that. Steve would probably say something about how she couldn't have been worth much or she wouldn't have chosen such an inconsiderate way to break the news to him, but Nick didn't want to hear Steve's opinion of anything, let alone of Lisa or Nick's judgment in dating her.

He drove past the theater where he'd hoped to take Lisa that evening, which was a mistake. He felt like a damned baby, wallowing in self-pity this way, and he swung the little Pinto around a corner. He'd drive by the mall, see if anything good was playing at the Tri-Plex there. Preferably something violent and heavy, with no girls in it, just guys slaughtering each other.

A group of young girls swarmed across the street when he stopped behind a truck at the crosswalk, giggling and horsing around. And then, just before the light changed, he saw a single figure step off the curb behind the others.

Dorky Daisy, he thought of her. The kid from next door. Every time he went out in the backyard she was hanging out a window calling down to him; if he went out the front, she would be sitting on her own front porch almost as if she were waiting for him. She'd bum a ride downtown, or ask to borrow the price of a movie, or show him a book she was reading.

To give her credit, Daisy always returned the money, and she read some pretty good books for a fifteen-year-old. Several of them he'd actually enjoyed.

Mostly, though, she was a pain in the neck. Larry teased him about her, which was irritating. He didn't want any of the kids from Sebastian High to see him with an undersized, carrot-headed, stringbean of a girl and think he was interested in her.

He was glad Daisy didn't spot the familiar Pinto. She looked lonely, hunched into her faded jeans jacket, as she headed across the mall parking area toward the theater.

Nick wasn't thinking about Daisy, though. There was a gang around the box office, some of them kids he knew, and he decided he didn't want to see any of them. Probably the news was already going around that Lisa Shafer had dumped Nick Corelli for a college man. Whatever the others thought about it, Nick didn't want to know. Not tonight.

He took a right, heading under the low overpass opposite the entrance to the mall, wishing he had somewhere to go until he could return home and go to bed. He didn't want to encounter either his mother's sympathy or his stepfather's judgment, even if Steve didn't put it into words.

And then it happened. There was no warning, nothing. The body fell onto the hood of the Pinto, then slammed into the windshield, face first. For what could have been no more than split seconds, Nick stared into the terror-filled eyes, and then the glass splintered and the face was gone.

He heard the scream of his own tires, heard tearing metal as the side of the car swiped the concrete abutment and came to a stop. He was so shocked that for long seconds he didn't move, staring at the ruined glass before him, watching a few shards of it fall inward, though most of it held.

"You all right? Hey, kid, are you hurt?"

A man had jerked open the passenger door—Nick's was wedged against the concrete wall—and was peering in. He looked at Nick's dazed face, then turned to yell over his shoulder. "Get an ambulance! Call the police!"

Nick couldn't think. Steve was the police, but he wasn't on duty now, was he? It wouldn't be Steve who came.

"Come on, kid, get out of there. This thing may burn—I can smell gas. Hurry up, release your seat belt!"

Numbly, Nick fumbled with the buckle. "What . . . did I hit something? I didn't hit anybody, did I?"

"You hit somebody, all right. I think he's dead." The stranger's hands reached for him, pulling him free of the wrecked car. Dad always said these little cars wouldn't be much protection in a wreck, and he was sure right. And I just got it paid for, Nick thought irrelevantly.

Because the car *was* irrelevant if he'd killed a man.

By the time he got out of the remains of the car, he was shaking so that he could hardly stand up. He heard sirens in the distance, and a crowd was beginning to gather, drawn from the late shoppers and moviegoers from the mall.

He probably knew a lot of them, but his vision was glazed. He was scarcely aware of the people.

When he turned a little, unwilling yet compelled to see, there was the man who had struck the car. He had slid off onto the street when the Pinto hit the concrete embankment, and he lay crumpled like a bundle of discarded rags.

"I couldn't have hit him," Nick said unsteadily. "I was only going about twenty miles an hour, I just came around the corner from Broad Street, and I never saw him. I never saw anything!"

The man who had urged him out of the car was kneeling beside the still figure.

"Don't touch him," another onlooker warned. It was Mr. Holtzmeyer from the bank, there with his wife dressed as if they were on their way to a dinner party, maybe. It was funny how some details—like the pearl necklace Mrs. Holtzmeyer wore, and the halo of blond hair highlighted by the streetlights that had just come on—stuck so sharply in Nick's mind, while everything else was so hazy.

He heard someone say—a girl's voice—"Hey, it's Nick Corelli!" but he didn't turn to see who it was.

"He's gotta be dead," the first man said, fingers seeking a pulse in the outflung wrist. "See how his head's twisted. Broke his neck, for sure."

Nick wondered if he were going to throw up. He steadied himself by putting a hand on the hood of the Pinto, then jerked back as his hand was slashed by a projecting band of metal. He saw the blood running freely and couldn't even think well enough to reach for a handkerchief to stop it until Mr. Holtzmeyer pressed one into his hand.

"It's the Corelli boy, isn't it? Mickey?"

"Nick." It was a wonder the man understood him, his lips were so numb. It didn't feel as if they moved when he spoke. He felt dizzy, and for a moment the streetlights seemed to dim.

"Here, come over here and sit down," Mrs. Holtzmeyer said. He'd always thought of her as stuck-up and cold, but she was nice enough now. Her hand on his arm guided him away from the car and the body—Nick no longer had any hope that it wasn't a *body*—and to a seat on the curb. "Put your head between your knees, that'll help."

He did as she said, not looking up even when the sirens died and he realized two police cars and an ambulance had pulled up alongside his own demolished vehicle. One of the cops put out flares and stopped traffic; the other one walked past Nick and stopped beside the dead man.

Dead man. Oh, God, Nick thought in despair, a dead man. How could it be? How had it happened?

"You the driver?"

Nick jerked his head up. He didn't recognize the officer standing over him. "Y-yes, sir."

"Your name, son? You got a driver's license?"

For a moment Nick couldn't think where the license would be, and then he pulled his wallet out of his hip pocket and flipped it open.

"Nicholas Corelli. Sergeant Macklin's stepson?"

"Yes, sir." Nick rose to his feet, staggering, and would have fallen if Mr. Holtzmeyer hadn't steadied him. "Is . . . is he really . . . dead?"

The nightmare had begun, and Nick couldn't think of anything to do about it, to make himself wake up and have everything be all right again.

He wished desperately that his dad were here, or even Mickey. Somebody. Somebody who could make it all right.

But there was nobody. Nobody but himself, Nick Corelli, and a dead man lying on the pavement.

3

The police were brusque and professionally efficient yet not unkind. Nick told his story to one of them and repeated it later to a second officer. That one told him, "I've called your folks. They'll be here to pick you up in a few minutes. They may want to take you over to the hospital and make sure you're not hurt."

"I'm OK," Nick said, though he'd never felt less OK in his life. He wished they hadn't called his mom and Steve, but it was too late now. He no longer felt as if he were going to throw up, but his legs were still trembling. He wondered if he should sit on the curb again, decided that sitting down would be less humiliating than falling down, and found a place where the wrecker blocked his view of what was happening to the stranger who had died on the hood of Nick's car.

The swirling colored lights from the top of the emergency vehicles almost made him dizzy. He wished they'd stop. Their flickering picked up answering color from something on the ground at his feet, and Nick

reached down without thinking to pick it up. Nothing but a chain someone had made from the pull-tabs from half a dozen beer cans. He sat twisting them between his fingers, staring into space without seeing anything.

"Nick? You OK?"

He turned as the girl in Levis and jean jacket settled onto the curb beside him. Her red-gold curls stirred in the breeze as she leaned forward toward him, concern evident on her face, her greenish eyes wide.

For once he didn't resent seeing Daisy. Anybody who was a friend, or sort of friend, was welcome in the present circumstances.

"Yeah, I'm OK." He kept saying that to everyone who asked, hoping that eventually it would be true.

"I was in line for the movie when I heard the crash," Daisy said. "Somebody said, 'Hey, that looks like Corelli's car,' and we all came across the street to see. Your hand's bleeding."

Nick lifted the stained handkerchief and stared at it as if he'd never seen it before. "Oh, yeah. I cut it on a sharp piece of metal that was sticking out. It's stopped bleeding. No big deal."

What *was* a big deal was that he'd killed a man, but he couldn't say that.

"They said he fell from the overpass," Daisy told him, as if reading his mind. "Charlie Sparks said he saw several guys talking up there when he first got into the ticket line. They'd parked their cars out at the end, there, and walked away from them. Charlie was joking about maybe they were making a drug deal or something, and didn't want to be overheard."

"Several guys?" Nick said dully. "Maybe one of them saw something. How could a guy fall from there? There's

a concrete rail that's waist high." He knew that because he'd often walked over the road there, taking a short-cut home from the mall.

Beside him, Daisy muttered a profane exclamation. "KCIZ just arrived," she said. "How lucky can we get?"

Nick swallowed at the sight of the familiar white van with the big call letters on the side of it, his stomach sinking. As if all this wasn't bad enough, now the whole mess was going to be on TV.

He had seen the young reporter on the evening news many times. Dark, glossily handsome, though when he had talked briefly to one of the police officers and then approached Nick, he wasn't as attractive as when he was on screen. His voice oozed professional sympathy. "Mr. Corelli? Nick, is it? I'm Gerry Stewart from KCIZ. Could you give us your version of what happened?"

Nick stared at him with loathing, remembering the interview Gerry Stewart had done with young parents whose children were trapped in a burning building. The words *your version* stung him at least partially out of this crippling paralysis. They seemed to suggest that what he would say would not necessarily be the truth.

Nick swallowed again and said thickly, "No comment, I'm afraid."

The TV reporter's dark brows arched. "No comment?" he echoed incredulously. "Sir—Mr. Corelli—a man has just been killed here!"

Daisy made a protective movement closer to Nick, so that their knees touched. "He's in shock, can't you see that? You can get the information you need from the police. Leave Nick alone."

The photographer behind the reporter moved in

for the kill, focusing on Nick's face, and Nick found himself wanting to strike out with a rock and smash the floodlight that was blinding him. Before he could repeat his refusal to discuss what he had no understanding of as yet—he'd lived with a cop long enough to know that many people said dangerously foolish things at moments like this, things they regretted; things that could be used against them in a court of law—Daisy spoke again.

"Hey, he's already told you! He's not going to talk about it!"

Would it come to that? Nick worried. Would he be charged with anything?

"Nick Corelli," the reporter was saying as the photographer maneuvered to get a shot from a different angle. "Aren't you related to Sergeant Macklin of the San Sebastian Police? Steve Macklin?"

"Hey, Gerry, Jim, better get a shot over here!" someone from the TV crew shouted, and to Nick's relief the reporter and the photographer gave up on him in favor of something more dramatic as the sheet-shrouded body was lifted into the ambulance.

"Ghouls," Daisy grumbled. "You OK, Nick?"

"I guess so," Nick said, wondering how long it would be before they let him go home. Wondering if his legs would hold him up to allow him to get there.

Up close this way, he could practically count the freckles on Daisy's small nose. He looked away, then wished he hadn't. The wrecker was moving, towing his Pinto to the junkyard, he supposed. The ambulance had already pulled out, but now that Nick's view was unobstructed he saw the spot where the victim had lain. It was marked by a dark stain that looked more black than red in the fading light, but he knew what it was, all right.

Nick fought down nausea. It must have shown on his face, because Daisy put a hand on his sleeve and urged, "Put your head down between your knees."

It had worked before, so Nick obeyed. Somehow the human touch—even dorky Daisy's—was welcome. God, how he wished his dad or Mickey would be coming to take him home!

It was pointless to think about that. It wasn't going to happen. After a moment Nick spoke, words muffled because his head was resting on his knees. "Did you hear anybody say what happened? Were there any witnesses?"

"I don't think so. The guy fell on your car. I heard one of the paramedics say he probably broke his neck when he hit and died instantly."

Nick kept his eyes closed. "Do you know who he was? Did anyone say?"

"Not that I heard. You couldn't help it, Nick, that he fell on your car. Nobody's blaming you."

He didn't bother to answer that. He simply sat there, silent and sick, until his mom and Steve showed up. He was glad Daisy stayed there, too, her hand resting on his arm, so he wasn't totally alone.

Elaine Macklin was still fussing, though less audibly, when they got home. How did you tell your mother you wished she'd just shut up and leave you alone, when you knew she meant well? Nick hadn't figured it out, but he had to bite his tongue to keep from yelling at her.

As soon as they were inside the house, though,

Steve helped. "I think maybe this is one of those times when some of your cocoa would be good for all of us, honey," he said.

"Yes, that's a good idea," she agreed at once, and vanished toward the kitchen.

Steve gave Nick a wry grin. "Sometimes the best thing you can do for a person is to give them something to keep them busy. Even if you don't want the cocoa."

"Yeah," Nick agreed. He wanted to get away from both of them, escape to the privacy of his own room, but he supposed if he went upstairs his mother would only bring the cocoa up there, and maybe then it would be hard to get her to leave.

Besides, right this minute he felt so wobbly he wasn't sure he'd make it up the stairs. Nick sank into the nearest chair.

Steve was watching him. "It's a rough experience, seeing someone die," he said quietly.

Nick swallowed, saying nothing.

"I remember the first time it happened to me. It was an old man who'd wandered away from a rest home and into the street; he got hit by a car just ahead of me. I tried to tell myself that he was ninety years old and probably wouldn't have lived much longer anyway, but it didn't help. He was a human being, and he probably wasn't any more ready to die than I was."

"This guy looked young," Nick managed, on the verge of tears.

"Probably around thirty, I guess. Age doesn't really matter. Seeing little kids hurt or killed bothers me the most. When I was with the Highway Patrol in Los Angeles I saw too many of those—it was the main reason I decided to find a small-town police force instead of sticking with the CHP," Steve said, sitting down on the couch opposite Nick. "Kids are the worst, but all death is difficult to handle. You never get used to it, no matter how often you see it."

"Do they know who he was?" Nick asked, his voice so low it was barely audible even to himself.

"Not yet, but they'll find out. Quite a crowd gathered, and no one recognized him, so he may not be local."

"Daisy said . . . Charlie Sparks saw a couple of guys standing up there on the overpass, talking. He thought maybe they were making a drug deal or something. He said they left their cars parked at the end, I guess there by the signs for the freeway. Maybe—maybe one of them saw something. Or one of them was *him*." He couldn't seem to stop swallowing. "I guess there weren't any witnesses. Nobody saw the guy fall."

"Not that we know of, so far. Someone may come forward with information tomorrow. I'll have them check out the business of the cars. Ah, here's our lady with the cocoa—with marshmallows, yet."

Nick didn't want it, yet he accepted the steaming mug, knowing his mother would only be further upset if he refused. He'd never figured out why she thought cocoa could cure *anything*, as if it were an antibiotic.

The heat felt good; he realized his hands were cold. As a matter of fact, he was chilled through. Did that mean he was in shock, maybe?

He made himself sip at the cocoa and it felt good going down, and in his stomach, too. It dawned on him that he'd never gotten as far as having supper, but he didn't want to mention it for fear his Mom would rush out to the kitchen and heat up some of the leftover liver and onions. He'd throw up for sure if she put a plate of *that* in front of him. No, that was a dumb thought. At a time like this, she'd never deliberately offer him something she knew he didn't like. Probably even Steve wouldn't do that.

His mother drank from her own cup while the three of them sat there in an uncomfortable silence. Then she glanced at her husband uncertainly. "Maybe I should call Stella and tell her we can't make it for pinochle tonight. What do you think?"

Steve opened his mouth, but before he could speak Nick said quickly, "Go ahead and go, Mom. You don't have to stay home because of me. I'm OK, really I am." Maybe if he said it often enough he'd believe it.

Steve was looking at him as if he saw through the facade and was evaluating his condition. "You sure, Nick?"

"Yeah. Honest. I'm shook up, but it isn't going to make any difference if you guys go on and play cards, the way you planned. I just want to . . . take a hot shower and go to bed."

Steve drained his cup and stood up. "OK. We'll be at Stella and Dale's until about midnight. Go on, honey, get your coat and let's go before they give up on us."

Some of the tension went out of Nick as he finished his own cup. At least they wouldn't be breathing down his neck all evening, giving him their amateur psychiatric therapy.

As he started up the stairs, he heard his mother say, "Do you really think it's wise to leave him, Steve?"

"Sure. He's going to handle it all right. I only wish

to God, though, that he'd stayed home and cleaned out the garage the way I wanted him to. Then he wouldn't have been under that damned overpass when the guy fell, or jumped, or whatever he did."

Jumped? That hadn't occurred to Nick before. Suicide? No, he thought, shuddering as he remembered that terrified face sliding toward him, slamming into the windshield—the man hadn't wanted to die.

He went on up to his room, wondering how Steve had meant his statement. Was it meant as criticism, that Nick hadn't done what Steve wanted? Or was it no more than an observation that didn't really mean anything?

Nick was confused and shaken, and not even a hot shower—he stood there until the hot water supply must have been almost depleted—made him feel all that much better. He wasn't shaking anymore, though, when he came out and shoved Dillinger off his bed so he could stretch out on it himself.

The little terrier gave him a reproachful look, which Nick ignored. After a moment Dillinger picked up an athletic shoe and brought it to the bed, pushing it against Nick's dangling hand.

"No, Dill. No walk right now. Lie down."

Dillinger hesitated, then softly deposited the shoe on the carpet and curled up beside it.

Once he was stretched out, Nick found it impossible to go to sleep. He wondered if Lisa had heard about the accident yet, if she'd call him. Now that he thought about it, he realized they'd been squabbling more than usual lately and that she'd been less sympathetic about his frequent, if minor, crossings of swords with his stepfather. Had she been giving him hints before today that their relationship was coming to an end?

If the accident had happened to *her,* he'd call her and express his condolences, he thought. But the house was silent. The phone didn't ring.

He couldn't stop thinking about what had happened, wondering who the man was, how he'd come to fall and break his neck. He'd have broken his neck anyway, if he'd hit the paving; why had he had to land on Nick's car?

Beside the bed in the darkened room—he had left on the hall light so that his mom and Steve wouldn't enter a dark house—Dillinger suddenly lifted his head, ears perking up.

Nick glanced at the clock and saw that it was only a quarter to ten. Too early for Mom and Steve to be coming back, unless his mother was going to fuss over him again.

Irritation, irrational but abruptly boiling over, brought Nick upright. If his mother came in one more time to assure herself that he was OK—what did she expect, that he'd be weeping into his pillow, or have hanged himself in the shower because he couldn't handle it?—he was going to lose it. He'd yell at her, or swear, or throw something. Why couldn't she understand that hanging over him this way drove him nuts?

Dillinger got up and padded out onto the landing. His tail started to wag, but it wasn't his mother's voice that Nick heard.

"Nick? You up there?"

His feet hit the floor with a thud. Daisy? What the heck was she doing here?

The overhead light glinted on her coppery hair as she poked her head around the corner. "Nick?"

"You taken up breaking and entering now, as well as being a Peeping Tom?" he asked, reaching for the lamp switch.

"The back door was unlocked. I just walked in. I figured if you were asleep, I'd go away. And if you were awake, I thought maybe you'd be hungry."

He saw now that she was carrying a tray with a cover over it, and though he'd have said a minute ago that food would nauseate him, the aroma coming from the tray set his salivary glands working overtime.

"What are you, my mother?" Nick asked, but he was less annoyed than he might have been.

"I know how I'd be feeling if I'd been through what you have," Daisy said, putting down the tray on the nightstand and lifting the cover.

"Starved, huh? What have you got?"

"I was fixing a snack for myself and decided maybe you'd like one, too. So I brought them both over here to eat. It's a guacamole-and-bacon burger. I hope you like onions. And my mom made brownies today. They're actually for a church bake sale tomorrow, but I snitched a few of them."

Nick was suddenly ravenous. He made no protest when Daisy sank onto the edge of his bed and reached for one of the hamburgers.

"Dig in," she said.

They chewed in silence for a few minutes, and Nick wished he'd eaten earlier. It made him feel better almost immediately. "Pretty good. Guess I'll try one of the brownies. If you didn't make them, they shouldn't poison me."

Daisy grinned. She looked rather like an elf, perched

cross-legged on the end of his bed. All she needed was a little green cap with a feather in it. "I guess it's true, what they tell women about how to handle men. My mom says if they're bleeding get out the bandages, and if there's anything else wrong with them, feed them."

At another time Nick might have been amused at her characterization of herself as a woman. As it was, he was simply grateful for the food. He ate his share of the brownies, which were even better than his mother's, and tossed the last bite, as usual, to Dillinger.

"I noticed you gave him the last of the hamburger, too. Does he always get it, no matter what you're eating?"

"Everything but broccoli. He won't eat broccoli. It's all gone, Dill." He held up his empty hands to prove it, and the dog reluctantly sank back onto the rug. "Now, Daisy, thanks for the food and the concern, and go home before my folks get here and find a girl in my room. My mom would have kittens."

Daisy slid obediently to her feet. "So would mine, if she knew I was here. Listen, Nick, it was awful what happened, but you're going to be OK, aren't you?" Her concern was obviously genuine and rather touching.

"Sure. Nobody thinks I killed the guy," Nick said. "Go on, beat it, before we get caught."

It was quiet once again after Daisy had gone. Nick followed her downstairs and locked the back door behind her. Steve had a real thing about locking doors and securing windows, though there was almost never any crime in this quiet neighborhood, except for kid stuff.

Daisy had always been a pest with an obvious crush on him, but he had to admit he was glad she'd come over tonight. Not just for the food, which had been great, but because talking to her for even a few minutes had helped a little. He thought he could sleep now.

He must have, for a short time, because he was aware of coming awake when Dillinger growled.

Growled?

Nick came wide awake, hearing the dog's toenails clicking on the wooden floor on the landing, and then, astonishingly, Dillinger barked.

Nick came up off the bed, still a little groggy. The clock on the nightstand said 11:06.

Dillinger had raced ahead of him, down the stairs, barking furiously.

Dillinger never barked when a member of the household came in, not even at Steve when it was in the middle of the night and he'd been working late.

Nick opened his mouth to call out, following Dillinger's fury toward the back of the house, when he was suddenly brought to an abrupt, heart-stopping halt.

From the kitchen came the sound of a shot, Dillinger's yip, and then silence.

4

Nick stopped, fingers on the switch that would flood the kitchen with light, not quite daring to proceed.

He'd heard gunfire often enough to be quite sure that a small handgun had just been fired inside the house. Joe Corelli had been a hunter, and Nick had often gone with him for both birds and deer.

There was no sound from Dillinger. Grief and rage began to build in Nick; he'd had Dillinger from the time he was eight weeks old and had made puddles on the floor and stolen his first forbidden shoe to chew.

If whoever the intruder was had deliberately shot the dog, would he hesitate to shoot Nick?

The kitchen was densely black; no light reflected anywhere. Belatedly, Nick realized that he himself was probably visible to anyone in the darkened kitchen, because that upstairs hall light spilled down, ever so faintly, into the dining room where he stood.

His heart was pounding and he felt suffocated, as if the air had suddenly grown too thick to breathe. He wanted to demand, "Who's there? What do you want?" but his throat worked soundlessly.

Dillinger, he thought in anguish. Don't be dead, Dillinger.

And then there was a rush of movement, more felt than heard, in the pitch-black room. A moment later, there came the sound of feet on the back porch, and the screen door slammed shut.

Nick had lost contact with the light switch and had to grope for it again. He blinked under the fluorescent flood of illumination.

"Dill!" Nick moved quickly to the little terrier's side, dropping to his knees beside his pet. "Oh, God, why did he have to shoot you?"

There was blood on Dillinger's head, and he wasn't moving. But when Nick laid his ear against the small chest, he thought he detected a heartbeat. Or was that only his own blood pounding in his ears?

Angrily Nick rose and grabbed for the wall phone. He didn't have to look up the number; his mother and dad had known Stella and Dale Harding for years, and their son Don had been one of Nick's friends since first grade.

"Mr. Harding? This is Nick Corelli," he said when he heard the voice on the other end of the line. "Somebody just broke in and shot Dillinger. Can I talk to Steve?"

Dale Harding muffled an exclamation, and a moment later Steve was on the line. "You hurt, Nick?"

"No, I'm fine, but I don't know about Dill." He heard, unashamedly, the hint of tears in his own voice. "The only wound I can see is in his head. He isn't moving."

"Dial 911 for the police. We'll be right there," Steve said, and hung up without saying good-bye.

Nick's hand was unsteady when he dialed, and his throat hurt when he relayed the required information to the emergency dispatcher. "We'll have an officer there at once," he was told calmly.

Nick went back to Dillinger immediately, though he didn't know what he could do. "Don't die, Dill," he said huskily, resting a reassuring hand on the little terrier, just in case Dillinger was aware of anything.

Steve and his mother got there by the time he heard the sirens. His mother's face was taut with alarm, but for once she didn't ask any frantic questions. Steve knelt briefly beside Dillinger, then spoke to his wife over his shoulder.

"Call the vet, tell him Nick's meeting him at the clinic with the dog. Here"—he tossed car keys at Nick as he stood up—"take my car. How did the guy get in? Wasn't the door locked?"

"Yes, it was. I locked it myself," Nick said, wondering what Steve would have said if there were no signs of forced entry, if Daisy hadn't alerted Nick to the unlocked door simply by walking in.

Then Nick looked at the keys in his hand, and for a moment he forgot about Dillinger. He was starting to shake again, just the way he had a few hours earlier at the scene of the accident.

"I—I don't know if I can drive—"

Steve's gaze bored into him, demanding, commanding. "You can drive. It's just like falling off a horse, Nick. You get up and ride again immediately. Otherwise you lose your courage ever to do it. You can't go through life without driving. Go on, I think the dog's still alive. If he was just creased enough to knock him out, he may be OK if you get him to the vet right away."

Elaine Macklin made a small sound and they both looked at her. "Do you want me to go?"

"Nick can tend to the dog. We'll need you here to tell us what's missing or out of place. Go on, boy!"

Steve had already turned his back, expecting him to obey. He was carrying one of those long Streamlite flashlights that cops use both for light and as a supplementary weapon; he stepped outside and grunted as he examined the door frame. "Used a crowbar, looks like. Elaine, come hold the light for me."

Nick's heart was beating more wildly now than when he'd nearly confronted the intruder in the darkness. The idea of driving so soon after the stranger had died in a fall onto his car made him physically sick to his stomach.

Yet there was Dillinger, lying on the vinyl floor, not moving.

Nick gulped and jammed the keys into a pocket, then gently gathered up the dog and headed out the front door, which still stood wide open as his mother had uncharacteristically left it.

Gently, he laid Dillinger on the passenger seat, then went around to the other side. His hand was so unsteady he could hardly get the key into the ignition.

It wasn't the same as getting back on a horse after you've fallen, he thought resentfully. He had been driving a car, and he'd killed somebody with it, only a few hours ago. For a moment he almost hated his stepfather for making him do this, when his mother could just as easily have come with him to drive, allowing Nick to hold the dog. She could have come back to answer their questions.

He turned the key and the engine of the almost-new Chrysler purred smoothly. He'd always wanted to drive it—it was a terrific car—but he'd never dreamed of doing it under these circumstances. He put it into reverse and carefully backed out of the driveway onto the deserted street.

He was nervous about the car and sick about Dillinger. He drove carefully, mindful of stop signs and cross traffic, thankful that Dr. Story's clinic was only a few miles away.

The vet drove up just behind Nick, hurrying over to unlock the door. "Got shot, your mother said? What happened, Nick?"

"Somebody pried open the back door, I guess. Dillinger was upstairs with me—I was asleep—and heard him, ran downstairs, barking. I heard the shot, and then the guy ran out the back door. Steve said it looked like the slug just creased his head, so maybe—"

He sort of strangled at that point, unable to put the rest of the thought into words.

"Bring him on back here," Dr. Story said, leading the way, turning on additional lights as he went.

Nick lowered the animal onto the stainless steel table, and his heart lurched with hope when Dillinger moved a little. "He *is* alive, isn't he?"

"Looks like it. Hold him, in case he comes around before I get through. Ah, it's all right, fella—hurts, I'm sure, but I think you're going to pull through if that's the only injury. It knocked him out, but he isn't bleeding too badly. You're sure there was only one shot?"

"Yeah. Just one. It was so close it made my ears ring." Now that Dillinger was coming around, licking at his hand, Nick felt like crying.

It wasn't until he was halfway home ten minutes later that he realized he hadn't even thought about starting the car and driving it until just that moment. Maybe Steve was right; maybe it had helped to drive again as soon as possible.

Dr. Story had suggested it would be best to keep Dillinger overnight for observation. "I'll take him home with me, make sure he's OK. You can pick him up in the morning around ten if there aren't any complications," he'd said.

When Nick eased the big car—it felt like the motorhome by comparison with his little Pinto—into the driveway and got out, he felt as if he'd just climbed the face of Half Dome at Yosemite. He was exhausted, mentally and physically, and he realized he needed another shower. He smelled terrible. He'd always heard that being scared could do that to you, and he'd sure been scared.

There were two police cars parked in front of the house. He heard the radio in one of them squawking as he went inside. A simple breaking and entering didn't usually justify two patrol cars in San Sebastian, not unless it was a slow night and the officers didn't have anything else to do so they came for the fun of it. After having Steve in the family for a few months, he knew most of the cops welcomed activity rather than uneventful shifts.

He wondered wryly, as he let himself into the house, if his mother was out there making cocoa for everybody. His dad used to laugh at what he called "Elaine's wonder drug," because she made cocoa to ease them through everything from skinned knees to failed exams.

She was in the living room, however, talking to a uniformed officer. "No, I can't see that anything at all was taken. I think the dog interrupted him before he could find anything. Oh, Nick! How's Dillinger?"

"Going to be all right, I think. Dr. Story's keeping him overnight, just in case. Did they find out how the guy got into the house?"

"Brute force," the officer said, turning as if to leave. "Just took a crowbar out of your own garage, looks like, and set to work to pry the frame off the door. Lucky it was the dog, not you, who surprised him."

Nick thought of those long seconds when he had stood in the kitchen doorway, silhouetted against the pale light from the upper hall. It could have been him rather than Dillinger with a bullet through him. It made him feel quite peculiar.

The officer was still standing there, and the other one came in from the rear of the house, with Steve following. "Aren't you the kid who was involved in that situation out by the mall where the guy was killed?"

Nick had, temporarily, forgotten that. "Yeah," he said.

"You've had some day," the officer said, almost in an admiring way. "Well, good-night, folks."

Nick watched them go. The officer didn't know the half of it. He hadn't heard about Lisa, and he seemed to be assuming that since Nick apparently wasn't being held responsible for the death of the stranger, that wasn't such a big deal, either.

His mother was looking at him. "You think you can sleep, honey? Do you want—"

Nightmare

"I don't want anything," Nick said hastily, before she could offer anything specific. "I'm going to hit the sack. See you in the morning, Mom."

He allowed her to give him a hug before he went upstairs, and even hugged her back. He knew she'd been scared when he called them home from their pinochle playing, but she'd kept her cool fairly well. Or Steve had warned her on the way home to act as if she had.

That last thought came as a surprise to him. Well, he thought, stripping off his sweat-soaked clothes for his third shower of the day, he had to admit that his mother had calmed down a lot since she'd married Steve. She didn't seem nearly as nervous or anxious. She smiled more. He'd even heard her singing as she went about her chores, something she hadn't done in those early months after her husband died.

I ought to count my blessings, Nick thought as he reached into the shower to adjust the water temperature. Steve asked if I was OK before he asked if I'd remembered to lock the back door.

He'd been mildly provoked with dorky Daisy for walking into the house without being invited, but he was glad now that she had. Otherwise, he'd have assumed someone else had locked the door, and there would have been no signs of forced entry, and Steve would probably have been furious with him.

The hot water was soothing as well as cleansing, and he stood under it as long as he dared before he turned off the water and reached for the towel.

He slept late. The sun was beating against the shade when he raised it the following morning, and it was unseasonably warm against his bare chest. He reached up for the sash to close the window and heard a familiar voice from the second story of the house next door.

"Nick! I thought you were never going to get up!" Daisy was leaning out her own bedroom window. "What was going on last night? I saw all the cops and I thought at first maybe they'd decided you murdered that guy and they were arresting you!"

"It wouldn't have been murder, since I don't even know who he is and never saw him before, and sure didn't mean to kill him," Nick pointed out. "If I'd hit him because I was careless, or driving too fast, it would have been vehicular manslaughter."

Daisy, halfway out the window onto the roof, shrugged. "Whatever. I wanted to come over and see what it was all about, but my dad wouldn't let me."

"Thank God for small favors," Nick said, preparing to close the window.

"No, wait! Hey, listen, tell me what it was, huh? It'll be in the paper, won't it? But I can't wait that late to find out!"

"If it makes the *Daily Globe,* it'll be three lines on page twelve," Nick predicted. "Breaking and entering, especially when they don't get anything, isn't exactly front page news."

"But I heard a shot! Didn't I? Who had the gun? Did you shoot at a burglar?"

"No. The guy who broke in had the gun. He shot Dillinger."

Even from the distance between their houses he thought he could see her turn pale. "Oh, no! Is he dead?"

"No, but he's at the vet's. I'm supposed to pick him up at ten."

Nightmare

"You've only got fifteen minutes," Daisy said, consulting her watch. "Hurry up and get dressed, and I'll go with you!"

Before he could open his mouth to protest, she had vanished from the window.

Nick swore, sighed, and closed his own window. He knew better than to mention to that girl in advance that he was going to go anywhere, or be anywhere. She'd embarrassed him more than once by asking for a ride home from a place he was sure she'd gone only because she knew he was going to be there. Once Lisa had said, "If she wasn't so little and skinny, and such a *child*, I'd wonder if I had something to worry about."

Well, Lisa wasn't worrying about him now. As far as he knew, nobody was, except maybe his mother, and he wished she'd stop.

To his relief he found her getting ready to leave the house on some errand of her own, instead of fluttering around him in the kitchen while he ate breakfast. "Jane Peart is picking me up in five minutes," she said. "My car keys are on the table, so you can get Dillinger. I've already spoken to Dr. Story, and he says Dill's going to be fine. We were really lucky; the shot could easily have killed him if it had been a fraction of an inch lower. I'll be gone until mid-afternoon, probably. You're all right, aren't you, Nick? It won't bother you to drive again after—"

"I'm fine," Nick said, and hoped he was right. Last night he'd been so busy worrying about Dillinger that he hadn't thought as much about the driving as he'd otherwise have done.

After she'd gone, he got out shredded wheat and milk and a banana, then made a couple of slices of toast with raspberry jam. He didn't have time for any more than that; he was going to run a little late meeting the vet as it was.

While he ate, he debated strategies to get rid of Daisy before concluding that it probably didn't matter if she went with him. It might make it easier on Dill if she held him on the way home.

She was waiting, leaning against his mother's four-year-old Montego, when he came out of the house. "This is a pretty car," she said, smoothing the dark red upholstery as she slid into the passenger seat.

"Yeah," Nick agreed. He turned on the ignition and decided that while he was still nervous, it wasn't as bad as it would undoubtedly have been before he'd driven Steve's car last night. "You can hold Dill on the way home."

She squirmed happily as she fastened her seat belt. "OK. How come you call him Dillinger? My dad said that's a crazy name for a dog."

"Your dad's a real diplomat," Nick told her, backing toward the street with more care than he'd normally have shown, telling himself that driving was no more difficult now than it had been before the accident, and it had never bothered him then. "We named him after a famous criminal, John Dillinger—"

"Dad said he was a mobster or something. What did your dog ever do to deserve being named after him?"

Nick eased around a corner and into the moderate Saturday morning traffic moving toward downtown. "The real Dillinger was a hoodlum who robbed banks, and when he was put in prison he kept escaping. When we first brought Dill home, Mom wanted to call him

Buddy, because that's what he was supposed to be for me, a buddy. Only we changed his name because it didn't quite fit. He kept swiping things. The first week he destroyed seven shoes, which Dad said had to be a record. And he took anything he found loose—keys, a pen, the newspaper—and hid it if he couldn't chew it up."

The Montego felt different from the Pinto, more solid, less likely to disintegrate if another car hit it. Or a body. No, Nick thought, he wouldn't allow that kind of thought to stay in his mind. Safer to talk about Dillinger.

"There was a while Mickey and I were afraid Mom wasn't going to let us keep him. After he swiped Dad's wallet and it was missing for three days, I wasn't sure even *Dad* was going to agree to keep him. Mick and I looked all over and finally found the wallet buried in the backyard, and we sweet-talked him into forgiving the puppy. And that was another thing." Nick felt he had to keep talking, so he wouldn't think about his driving.

"Terriers are natural-born diggers. Dill could dig his way out of any yard or pen we were able to devise, short of a concrete run, which at that time Dad said we couldn't afford to build. One day Grandpa Corelli came over and brought in a handful of letters because he'd met the mail carrier. He made the mistake of putting them down on the coffee table, and Dill stood up on his hind legs and pulled them all down. He raced away with an envelope that had a check in it, and by the time we got it back his teeth had punched a lot of holes in it. Grandpa said he was more of a hood than a buddy, that he was like one of those old-time criminals, John Dillinger or Al Capone. Mickey got him telling stories about those days, and the next time Dill stole something, Mick started calling him Dillinger. It stuck. It looks like Doc Story just got here, too, so I didn't keep him waiting after all."

He pulled in behind the vet's car and got out, Daisy right behind him. "How's he doing, Dr. Story?"

"He's probably got a nasty headache, but he drank water, and I suspect he'll eat when you offer him food. Take it easy for another twenty-four hours, though. Keep it light, and not too much of it. Come on inside, I'll give you a prescription for the next couple of days, for pain."

Dillinger seemed happy to see them, licking first Nick's hand and then Daisy's chin as he was given into her care for the ride home.

On the way there, Nick had to submit to a detailed interrogation, first regarding the incident in which Dillinger had been shot, and then about the accident. Talking to Daisy wasn't the same as talking to his mother or Steve—who tended to sound like a cop no matter who he was talking to, except for Elaine. Daisy was simply curious and not unduly sympathetic or fussy.

He was afraid she was going to try to follow him into the house with the dog, but her mother called from the adjoining yard as they got out of the car.

"Daisy, I told you, you've got to clean your room before Aunt Wilma gets here!"

"OK, I'll be right there," Daisy called back. She made a face at Nick. "My great-aunt. She's about eighty, and she's going to stay three weeks, and she can't stand noise. Not even music. *Especially* not music, not my kind, anyway. And she's going to get my room, and I'm going to have a sleeping bag in Daddy's study."

"Daisy! *Right now!*"

Daisy grimaced and handed over Dillinger. "See you," she said, and ran, yelling over her shoulder. "I hope all the bad stuff is over!"

Nick didn't even bother to say, "It is now that you're going home," as he might have in the past. He carried Dill into the house, and he, too, hoped the bad stuff was over.

5

I t *was* over, Nick thought. The accident was behind him and nobody was blaming him for it; his relationship with Lisa was ended. His car was totaled, but Dillinger was practically back to normal. Steve had finally gotten off his back about cleaning the garage after Nick spent an afternoon straightening it out.

He'd had the worst few days of his life, except for when his dad was dying. Undoubtedly Steve was right. It was time he put all the catastrophes out of his mind and picked up the pieces.

Or at least pretended to. If he acted normal, maybe everybody'd start treating him as if it were true. It would help if the dreams would stop, though. He didn't know what he could do about those except hope that he wouldn't make enough noise to wake his mother or Steve during the nightmares.

He would try for all he was worth to be normal, on the inside as well as on the outside.

But that very day, Tuesday, he flunked a calculus test.

Nightmare

Mr. Traynor called him up as the rest of the students were leaving the room. "What happened, Nick? I expected a strong B+ out of you at the lowest, maybe even an A."

Nick licked his lips, wondering how much this would affect his final grade. "I don't know. I just couldn't seem to think straight. I couldn't keep my mind on it."

Mr. Traynor studied him for a moment. He was a short, pudgy man with a prematurely balding head, but he was a great math teacher. "Did it have anything to do with what happened Friday night? I read about the accident. Very tragic. And then I understand your house was broken into and your dog was injured. You've had a bad few days."

"Yeah." Nick cleared his throat awkwardly. Mr. Traynor didn't know the half of it. Didn't know about Lisa, who didn't meet his eye when they passed in the halls, who ate lunch at the next table over from Larry and Nick, and giggled over her weekend with the big Harvard man loudly enough for Nick to make out most of the words. "I guess I was kind of . . . spaced out, or something. I didn't sleep much last night. I kept having this nightmare—" He stopped, not wanting to seem like a crybaby.

Mr. Traynor considered the matter. "Do you think you could do better if you took it again? Under the circumstances, I think that might be allowable. You're one of my best students, and you have been through a rather traumatic time."

It hurt when he swallowed. "I'd appreciate another chance, if it's possible."

Deliberately, Mr. Traynor tore the test pages in two and dropped them into the wastebasket. "Officially, you didn't take the test today. In case you're not aware of it, that's against the rules, but in my judgment these circumstances warrant bending them a little. I'll meet you here on Friday morning at six o'clock—can you manage that?—and we simply won't mention it to anyone else. Your grade will go into the book at that time. If anyone wants to know why we're here so early, we are working on an extracurricular project that won't be explained."

Nick felt a surge of gratitude, which he expressed as best he could. The good feeling even carried him through a face-to-face meeting with Lisa on the way out, and he took a little satisfaction from seeing that she was embarrassed by his direct look. His feelings about her were confusing. On one hand, he was angry and resentful at the way she'd ended their relationship, while on the other, he hurt, wishing they were still together.

Several other girls had gone out of their way to speak to him, and he knew the news was out that he and Lisa had split up. He supposed that if he immediately found another girlfriend it would help the talk to die down sooner. But he wasn't ready for that yet.

Daisy was sitting on his front steps when he got home for supper, holding a newspaper. Nick felt a surge of annoyance. It had been a mistake to let her go with him to pick up Dill, a mistake to talk to her beyond the brief remarks that he'd been using before that to fend her off. He didn't dislike her, but he didn't want her coming over all the time, either. Even Larry would start making smart remarks if he knew how much Daisy was hanging around. She looked, at the moment, in her worn jeans and plaid shirt, as if she were twelve years old.

She lifted her head eagerly when she heard his

approach. "Have you seen it yet?"

"Seen what?" Nick asked, in spite of his resolve to give her no encouragement or excuse to stick around.

"Tonight's paper. They identified that guy. It's here, on page three."

Nick felt as if somebody'd just landed a karate kick in his groin. He didn't have to ask who "that guy" was.

Daisy moved over to make room for him on the top step, the newspaper opened and refolded on her knees. Without really meaning to, Nick sank down beside her. Daisy had circled the story with a pencil, and now she pointed it out with a slim finger.

Nick's eyes read the headline DEAD MAN IDENTIFIED before his vision blurred. It didn't matter, Daisy was interpreting it for him. She'd make a great Seeing Eye dog, he thought, trying for composure.

"I practically know it by heart already. You want to read it, or shall I just give you the gist of it?" She didn't wait for him to respond. "His name was Paul J. Valerian, and he was thirty-one years old. He came from Galveston, Texas, and the night before he was killed stayed in the West End Motel." She quoted: "'Manager Richard Gobles, 56, said Valerian checked in with one small bag, paid in cash, and seemed quiet and perhaps depressed. He didn't want to talk to the motel employees or other guests.'"

Daisy shot a glance at him from beneath thick auburn lashes. Nick was struggling to control the gut reaction to having a name put to the man who had died. It made him more real, a person rather than a stranger; suddenly Nick didn't want to know any more about him, but he couldn't stop her.

"It says they found evidence on the overpass indicating that he had stood there for some time before he jumped over the railing and landed on—"

"Jumped?" Nick echoed. "What do you mean, jumped? Did anyone see him do that?"

"No, it says no witnesses. But there were cigarette butts that suggested he had been there long enough to smoke about half a pack. I didn't get that from the article in the paper, but Jill Milton's mom works in the typist pool at the police station, and that's what she said."

"I thought such things were supposed to be confidential; classified, or something," Nick said hollowly.

"Well, if it was a murder case or something, I guess it would be. But this is just a guy who jumped off an overpass and killed himself."

Nick's breath caught in his chest. "Killed himself? They're saying he killed himself? By jumping onto my car?"

"Rotten thing to do, all right," Daisy said. "Inconsiderate, to say the least."

"No way," Nick said before he knew he was going to say it. "I saw that guy's face—and I see it again, every night in my dreams—and he didn't want to die. Maybe he knew he was *going* to, but he didn't want to. He didn't deliberately jump."

"Maybe he changed his mind on his way down," Daisy suggested. "I mean, if he'd really intended to die, why would he stand around smoking all those cigarettes? Getting up his nerve to do it, maybe? And then, when he realized it was going to, you know, really hurt when he landed, he changed his mind. After it was too late."

"They figured out he killed himself, just from a few cigarette butts? I don't believe it."

"It says 'evidence.' Maybe there was other stuff, too. It doesn't say he left a note or anything like that. They found his car a block from the motel. He went walking and saw the overpass and figured it was as good a place as any to do it."

"Baloney." The word was emphatic, and Daisy twisted to look into his face.

"It could have happened that way, Nick."

"It would be a stupid way to kill yourself. That overpass isn't even very high! If he hadn't landed on my car, if he hadn't broken his neck, he might not have died at all! If you're going to commit suicide by jumping, you jump off a tall building or something like the Golden Gate Bridge."

"There aren't many tall buildings in San Sebastian. And the Golden Gate is in San Francisco."

"Then why didn't he go to San Francisco? It's only another four hours' drive, and he could have done it right. If he came all the way from Texas, what was he doing here anyway?"

"I guess they didn't find any connection with anybody here. It says his family in Galveston has been notified and that his body will be taken there for burial."

"His family?" Nick felt stricken. "He had a family?"

"Most people have relatives. He wasn't just hatched out of an egg. It doesn't say anything about who they were."

"It was bad enough when it was just him who died," Nick said, fighting nausea. "Now I have to think about his parents, or maybe a wife—maybe kids—" His eyes were stinging again, the way they had when it had happened.

"But it wasn't your fault. If he did it himself, why should you keep feeling guilty?"

Nick drew in a deep breath, hoping more oxygen would help. "I don't know. I just do. And I can't believe it was suicide."

"What else could it be? You said yourself that even though there's no protective high fence like on the freeway overpasses, the railing is high enough so nobody'd be likely to fall over by accident. What do you think happened if he didn't commit suicide? Do you think he was murdered?"

Daisy was perfectly serious. Nick clenched his hands into fists to keep the tremor in them from showing. "I don't know," he said helplessly. "It's just hard to believe that if he wanted to die, he would have looked so . . . terrified."

"Daisy! Supper!" The shout from next door brought their heads around.

Daisy grimaced. "Aunt Wilma's a health nut. She doesn't like anything good. I don't suppose we'll have a decent meal the whole time she's here. She wants wheat germ on everything, and *no sweets.* Even Daddy's getting tired of it already; he sneaked me a Milky Way last night."

"She and Steve might get along," Nick said, trying to pull himself out of the enveloping miasma of depression. "He likes liver."

Daisy stood, poised for flight. "No. Aunt Wilma only eats fish and poultry. No red meat or organ meats."

"You better go," Nick said. "Your mom's coming out of the house again."

"Yeah. See you later," Daisy said, and ran across the lawns between their houses.

Nightmare

He was in a lousy mood when he entered his own house. Even chicken and dumplings—his mom was a great cook—didn't help.

The man who had died now had a name. Paul Valerian. He had a home—Galveston. And he had a family, who were paying to have his body shipped home so they could bury him.

Everything Nick had said about suicide was true. Had the police made any attempt to find out why Paul Valerian was here in San Sebastian, a small California town? Had they figured out any reason why he'd want to kill himself?

Or—the thought came unbidden, unwanted—why anyone else might have wanted to kill him?

The word hung there in his mind for the rest of the evening, while he did his homework, while he half watched a stupid sitcom. It was still there when he went up to bed.

Murder. That was something you heard about all the time on the six o'clock news, but it didn't happen in a town like San Sebastian. It happened in places like San Francisco and Los Angeles. And it didn't touch the lives of ordinary people like Nick Corelli.

Was murder a possibility?

The thought was suddenly there in his mind as he lay in his dark room: *I wouldn't feel so responsible if I knew someone else actually killed him.*

Not that Nick wanted it to be murder. However it had happened, the man was dead. A young man, who ought to have had years yet to live. And the idea of family in Galveston gnawed at Nick. A part of him wished the paper had said what family he had: parents, brothers and sisters, a wife. Children. But that would make the reality even more stark than it was now, so another part of him wished the paper hadn't mentioned family at all. Family meant people who cared about you, who suffered when you died. The way he and his mom and Mickey had suffered when Dad died.

He wasn't ashamed of crying a little then, lying in bed late at night. Crying for the family that had been his own, that was now split up. Dad was gone, Mickey was far away, and though Nick and his mother still lived in the same house, it wasn't the same, because now her loyalty was split between Nick and Steve, and he knew that most of it went first to her husband.

Whatever the truth about the incident, it wasn't his fault, Nick told himself. He had a chance to make up that important test, to keep an F from pulling his grade down. He had to stop thinking of things that distracted him from studying, from concentrating on the test itself. He would refuse to think about the stranger who had died. It was over, it was past, and the only sensible thing to do was to go on from here. There was nothing else he could do, actually.

Yet it was impossible to put the matter entirely out of his mind. When kids at school looked at him oddly, he knew they were wondering about it. A few of them had expressed sympathy in an awkward fashion, but mostly they just gave him those looks.

It continued to hurt that after he and Lisa had been so close for months, she didn't talk to him at all. On Wednesday, she murmured "Hi," when they passed in the corridors, but she made no attempt to say anything about what had been in the papers, what everyone in town had heard about. It would have helped, a little, if she had.

That night he had a blowup with his stepfather.

Afterward, when he tried to tell Larry about it, he wasn't even sure how it had begun, nor why it had accelerated into an actual confrontation.

They'd eaten dinner together, the three of them, with Dillinger waiting expectantly on his rug in the corner. (When Dad was alive, Dill had sat beside Nick's chair, causing no problems, but though Steve liked dogs, he didn't believe in having them beg at the table.) Although Steve seldom talked much about his work, tonight he recited a story about an incident that had taken place that day when an old Scout, driven by one of a trio of drunks, had run up a telephone-pole guy wire and left the vehicle on its top and the occupants too befuddled to open the locked doors so that rescuers could get them out.

The fact that Steve had mentioned anything to do with police work, even as remotely connected as a minor traffic accident, gave Nick a burst of bravery, and he asked about the evidence that had led to a verdict of suicide in the case of Paul Valerian.

"I heard there were cigarette butts on the overpass, as if he'd stood there for a while, but that's not strong enough to prove anything, is it?"

Steve finished chewing a bite of round steak before he replied. "No, but there were other things. The few people who remembered him—the motel manager, a maid who cleaned his room, a waitress where he ate several meals—all had the impression he was upset, depressed. Nervous, restless. There was a half-finished letter to his wife in the motel room—"

His wife. Nick felt his guts knot painfully.

"—and while it wasn't a suicide note, it showed a frame of mind that might have been suicidal. He was concerned for her if anything happened to him, that kind of thing. Sort of as if he *expected* something to happen. Falling accidentally from up there would have been practically impossible. Otherwise the city fathers, or some of our good citizens, would have insisted on a chain link fence, like the ones we put on the freeway overpasses."

Nick's mouth was dry and he no longer wanted anything to eat. "Did they consider that he might have been . . . pushed, rather than jumping?"

Steve buttered another slice of bread. "I'm not on the case, but I'm sure they considered all the possibilities. The guy was in good physical condition, reasonably well dressed. He and his car were both clean; nothing to suggest involvement with drugs or anything like that. He was carrying about seventy dollars and a gasoline credit card, and he hadn't been robbed. There were no toxic substances in his body: no drugs, no alcohol. Quit worrying about it, Nick. It was just bad luck on your part that he fell onto your car. Nobody thinks you had anything to do with it except happening to be at the wrong place at the wrong time. You've got nothing to feel guilty about."

"Did the police find out who the men were, standing on the overpass just a minute or so before it happened?" Nick persisted, unable to let it drop.

"Like I said, I'm not on the case. I'm sure they investigated everything that was there. I didn't hear any scuttlebutt about mysterious guys hanging around, so there couldn't have been anything important. Let it go, Nick. It isn't exactly dinner-table conversation matter."

Nick fought against resentment, struggled to keep his voice level, neutral. "When is a good time to talk about something that bothers me? This is the only time we usually sit down together. You're the only one I know who has any of the answers."

"I just told you, I *don't* have the answers. The department and the medical examiner are satisfied the guy jumped. Case closed."

"I know I should have stopped there," Nick told Larry later, "but this thing is driving me crazy. So I asked him if they tried to find out why this Valerian guy was in San Sebastian, why he was even in California. And Steve put down his fork and spoke to me as if I were a little kid having a temper tantrum instead of an adult asking a perfectly reasonable question about something important. He said the case was closed and to *forget* it. I felt like yelling that I *can't* forget it, that I keep having these damned nightmares and going through the whole thing again practically every night. I opened my mouth— I don't even know what I was going to say—and Steve said, 'Finish your supper,' and I said I couldn't eat, and for some reason even *that* made him mad. I got up and left the table, and he yelled after me—"

It was still upsetting to him the next day as he related it all to Larry. "I kept on going and heard my mom trying to calm him down. She sort of apologized this morning, said he was under a lot of pressure about something to do with his job, that he was sorry he'd flared up that way. *He* never apologized. Honest to God, Larry, I don't know how I'm going to make it in that house through the rest of this year and two more years at junior college, living at home."

Only Dillinger was the same as he'd always been. His head injury healed rapidly. The little terrier slept beside Nick's bed (or on it if he got away with it) and licked a hand or a cheek that was close enough to the edge for him to reach.

Late Thursday afternoon, Mickey called.

"What's up?" Nick asked, basking in a wave of pure pleasure—well, no, there was a yearning to see his brother there, too—as he leaned against the wall, prepared for a good visit.

Mickey was his usual ebullient self, enthusiastic about working on Uncle Ben's ranch, riding horses, the girl named Brenda. He went on at some length about Brenda and had Nick laughing in spite of himself. "I miss you, buddy."

"I miss you, too," Nick said, and felt the prick of tears.

"How's old Dillinger doing? Mom wrote that somebody broke into the house and shot him!"

"Yeah, creased his skull. He's OK now. Still swiping things and eating my last bite of everything. He bugs Steve sometimes, I guess; but after the way he defended the house against a burglar, I think Steve'll give him some latitude. More than he gives me, actually."

Mickey's voice turned serious. "You and Steve not getting along yet?"

"Not the greatest," Nick told him. "I sure wish you were still home, Mick. It would help, having the two of us together again."

"Yeah. Hey, spring break's coming up, isn't it? Why

don't you come see me? You'd have time to drive to Houston if you didn't dawdle. We'd only have a day or two, but it would be better than nothing. Get you away from home while you're off school, so you'd lessen the friction with Steve. What do you think?"

The idea sent a spasm of emotion through him. "Gosh, I'd love to, but my Pinto was totaled after the guy fell on it and made me ram it into a cement wall. I don't know if it would have held up for that long a trip, anyway."

"What about the motorhome? Mom said she'd decided to sell it, but it's still there, isn't it? Hey, Nick, think about it, seriously! It would be great seeing you!"

A longing so intense it was almost painful swept through him. "Break's next week. But they probably wouldn't let me go."

"Why not? Dad taught you to drive the thing when you were only barely old enough for a driver's license, and he said you were a natural driver. You took the wheel plenty of times when we were out on a trip, and you never had any trouble. Ask, kid! You know, Steve might like the idea of having you out of the house for a week or so even more than you'd like to get out—give him privacy with Mom, something he's never had much of, so far. Since I met Brenda I'm beginning to realize that it can't be so great to marry a gal and not have any time alone with her. Ask, Nick! I don't see any reason why they wouldn't let you come!"

The idea had never occurred to him to drive to see Mickey in the motorhome. He was pretty sure Steve would veto any such proposal, but Nick knew he wanted badly to go.

He swallowed audibly. "Well, I'll ask. I'll call you back when they say, whichever way."

He'd have asked immediately, but his mom and Steve weren't there. He'd come home a little early for a change, and they'd gone grocery shopping together. Nick wondered, unexpectedly, if even such a mundane errand was a treat for them because they got to do it by themselves. Away from him.

Nick swore, making Dillinger perk up inquiring ears. "Nothing, Dill. Nothing's wrong," he said, though in truth quite a bit *was* out of kilter. "You want out? OK, come on."

He locked the door after he'd let the little terrier out, then went upstairs. His room felt stuffy, and he decided to open a window to freshen the air. He had to study for that test in the morning, and maybe extra oxygen would help.

When he opened the window, he heard a voice in the backyard and looked down to see Daisy feeding Dillinger something out of a yellow bowl.

"Hey! Why are you poisoning my dog?"

Daisy looked up and grinned. "He likes leftovers," she said.

"You're seducing him," Nick accused. "He shouldn't be eating food from strangers."

"I'm not a stranger," Daisy said happily. "We got to be friends when I carried him home from the vet's."

Nick made a sound of disgust and turned away from the window. Even Dillinger was turning out to be a traitor, he thought.

But maybe, just maybe, his folks would let him go visit Mickey over spring break.

He opened his calculus book and began to study.

6

To Nick's total astonishment, they agreed to let him go.

It wasn't an immediate decision. Steve's initial reaction was negative—was that simply part of being a cop, Nick wondered, because he was so used to dealing with negative situations?

"That thing's nothing for a kid to drive," Steve said, a frown beginning to form, but Elaine interjected quickly, "Why not? Joe taught both the boys to drive it as soon as he got it, and Nick's an excellent driver. Even I have driven the coach a little, on back country roads, and you know what a pansy *I* am. It handles beautifully. It's really safer than a car, because you're sitting up high, as if you're in the cab of a truck, and you can see trouble developing ahead of you much better than from a car. And it would be wonderful for the boys to get together. They've missed each other a lot since Mickey went to Texas."

"Besides," Nick said, making himself look directly at his stepfather, "it would give you two some time to yourselves. This last week's been pretty stressful. Seems like we could all use some space."

Steve hesitated, looking at his wife. "You really think he can handle it? Going all that distance?"

Nick wanted to ask what difference the distance made; if he was a competent driver, and the vehicle was sound, the number of miles was immaterial.

"Mickey drove that far," Elaine reminded him gently, "in *his* old car."

"And broke down before he got there," Steve pointed out.

"But as soon as we wired him the money for a new carburetor, he installed it himself and made it to Ben's," Elaine said. "And Mickey's car was eight years old. The motorhome is in excellent mechanical shape. There's no comparison, Steve. Let's let Nick go."

Afterward, Nick was convinced that the persuading argument was getting rid of him for a week or ten days. He didn't care—at least not much—as long as they let him go.

"You want to come along?" he asked Larry when he told him half an hour later.

Larry spread his hands in a gesture of helplessness. "I can't, Nick. My dad's got me painting the house during spring break! He's even going to pay me. I wouldn't skip the trip for that alone, but he'd never agree. Not with Mom screaming about the house having to look good for Jake's wedding. I don't know why *our* house needs to look fancy, Jake's only the groom, and it's the bride who counts, right?—except that relatives are coming to stay overnight. But she's worn Dad down, and he'll be sitting on me."

Nightmare

"I guess it's just you and me, then, mutt," Nick said, scratching behind Dillinger's ears. "Let's get the coach loaded, and I'll take off Friday night, get as far along the road as I can before I have to sleep."

"Out of California and heavy traffic, anyway," Larry agreed, looking wistful. "Will Bob give you the time off?"

"Yeah. I stopped there on the way over here. He said I haven't been worth a lot since the accident anyhow, and it would probably do me good. It's funny, you know, I could hardly stand the idea of driving again after it happened, but Steve made me, and now—well, driving the motorhome is different, somehow. I'm not worried about driving *that.*"

"Stay out from under overpasses," Larry advised, and Nick managed to laugh with him. There would be quite a few underpasses between San Sebastian and Houston, and he hoped he wouldn't freak out when he came to them. Probably it was like Steve had said: The sooner he tackled them, the quicker he'd get over his apprehensions.

It was dark when he started home. He'd gotten so used to running around in the Pinto that it was awkward having to do everything on foot, and he'd forgotten how long it took him to get from one place to another that way.

He decided to throw his clothes together that night and start filling up the refrigerator and the freezer compartment in the motorhome. He wouldn't need much to wear except a few jeans and shirts and some underwear. Food was what might take a little more time. A guy got hungry driving long distances. And dog food. He'd have to put in some dog food; he'd already decided

69

to take Dillinger with him for company, since Larry couldn't go and there wasn't anyone else he wanted to invite.

Dillinger trotted along beside him on the way home, perky as if nothing had happened to him. "I bet you'll be glad to see Mickey, too, Dill, won't you?"

Dillinger looked up at him questioningly upon hearing Mickey's name, wagging his tail a little.

"You want to go see Mickey?" Nick asked as they passed under a streetlight. Dillinger barked and leaped around his feet, almost tripping him. There was no doubt that Dillinger knew whom he was talking about. When Mickey was at home, each had sent the dog after the other one. "Go wake up Mickey," Nick would say, or it would be "Go fetch Nick."

As he turned onto his own street, he heard sirens. A police car went screaming past, much to Dillinger's excitement. Nick picked him up and carried him rather than risk having him run on ahead by himself.

"Getting to be just like the big city here in San Sebastian," he said, hugging the little terrier against his chest. "Cops and robbers all over the place."

The police car rolled in to the curb, heading the wrong direction, and a uniformed officer got out of the car, moving swiftly. Another car was approaching from the opposite direction and slid in nose-to-nose with the first one.

Nick sucked in a breath when he saw where the police cruisers were: in front of his own house.

"What the heck—"

He put Dillinger down now, because there were no more intersections to cross, and broke into a run.

Nightmare

The neighbors were appearing on their lawns. Mrs. Bascombe was so intrigued she'd come out without her wig, which in itself was attracting some attention. The Kellys were standing in their yard across the street, openly staring, and there was a slight, familiar figure silhouetted against the flashing red and blue lights.

"Daisy? What's going on?"

She spun, colliding with the explosive furry animal who was delighted to see her and confused and excited by the police cars and officers. "Nick! I'm glad you're here! I called the cops because I saw this guy going in your bedroom window! I thought at first it was you, maybe you forgot your key or something, but then when he turned on the light inside I got a better look at him, and he's not as well built as you are, nor as tall! You got a key on you, so the cops can get in?"

She was more excited than Dillinger was. Her fair skin was mottled blue and red from the revolving lights, her lips parted, her eyes shining. Obviously Daisy was enjoying this more than she was frightened by it.

One of the officers was coming toward them; Nick saw that he was one who had been here before, the night Dillinger had been shot. "Can you give us a key?" he asked.

"Sure." Nick fumbled for his key ring. "I'll let you in. Is he still in there?"

"We don't know. You and the girl stay out here. If he's in there and armed, we don't want to worry about you being in the way. Why don't you go up on the porch over at your house?" he addressed Daisy, but he didn't wait to see what they did.

"How good a look at him did you get?" Nick demanded, reluctant to move as far away as Daisy's house.

"Not real good. I mean, when I saw him going up onto the low part of the roof he was just a shadow. He didn't move like an athlete, either, now that I think of it. I mean, I've watched you move enough so I know how graceful you are. He was awkward getting over the windowsill. I couldn't tell much after he was inside, though. Just that he was shorter and kind of thin. Not very big through the shoulders. Cripes, what have you got in your house that makes everybody want to burgle it?"

"Nothing that I know of." It had just occurred to Nick that his bedroom window had been unlocked. It was on the second floor and he had never felt any need to lock it, since he kept opening it so often. Would Steve be ticked off because it had been easy to get in that way?

About that time Steve drove up, unable to use the driveway because it was blocked by one of the police cars. He came boiling out, heading for Nick and Daisy as soon as he saw them.

"Nick? You OK? I picked up the call on the radio. The guy still in there?"

"Nobody knows yet. They just took my key so they could go in. There's another cop around the back."

"Stay here," Steve instructed, and moved purposefully after the uniformed officers.

Five minutes later, they were allowed to enter the house. The intruder, whoever he was, had gone. Probably, Steve said, through the downstairs bathroom window, which was still open, the screen knocked off. "That window is hidden by the hedge from Mrs. Bascombe's. He probably ran when he heard the sirens and went out the back alley. Todd's taking a look out there now."

"Does it look like he got anything?" Nick asked.

"You'll have to decide that. As far as we can tell, the only place he trashed was your room."

"My room?" Nick was bewildered. "What the heck did he want in my room? I haven't got anything valuable. Even my tape player is an old one of Mickey's. No self-respecting fence would make an offer on it. I had my wallet on me." He patted his back pocket just to make sure.

"Well, better take a look, see if you can spot anything that didn't occur to me. I thought this was supposed to be a low-crime neighborhood, but I'm beginning to wonder."

Nick headed for the house, and Daisy bounced along beside him. "Can I come, too? Can I see what he did?"

Nick gave her a resigned glance. "You didn't just turn in that alarm to see some action, did you? You got a thing about cops and colored lights?"

"Everybody'll ask me tomorrow, since I live right next door to you," Daisy said, skipping to keep up with his longer strides. "I might as well have the details right. Right?"

It was a peculiar feeling, entering his own home, knowing that some hostile stranger had violated their privacy, perhaps endangering any family member who might have been home.

On that thought he turned toward Steve, who had entered behind them. "Where's Mom? She wasn't here, was she?"

"No, she's at a Tupperware party at Helen Martin's.

Check out your room, Nick, then tell us if anything is missing."

Daisy moved ahead of him up the stairs and was the first one to reach his bedroom door. She stopped so that Nick stepped on her heels, and the expletive she used was not one he was used to hearing from girls.

Nick was too shocked at what he saw over her shoulder to give a second thought to such a sweet-faced little girl using such language. His own exclamation was even worse.

"When your dad said your room had been trashed," Daisy said in awe, "he wasn't kidding, was he?"

"My stepdad," Nick said automatically, but he wasn't thinking about Steve.

The mattress had been pulled off the bed, the sheets and blankets thrown carelessly over a chair. The dresser drawers had been pulled out and left in a heap on the floor. Books had been tumbled out of the bookcases; pictures had been knocked off the walls; cassette tapes were scattered out of their case, on top of everything else. The closet door stood open, pockets turned inside-out on two jackets Nick could see, most of the rest of the things that had been on hangers thrown into a confused mass on the floor.

One of the uniformed officers stepped to the doorway behind him, along with Steve. "Might have been looking for drugs. Something small enough to fit into a pocket, from the look of it."

Nick spun angrily around. "There's no reason anyone would expect to find drugs in my room. Or our house."

"Nick's right," Steve said quietly. "If my kid was on something, I assure you I'd have picked up the clues.

Money's more likely. Maybe money to buy drugs. Not too logical for anyone to expect to find much cash here, but if he was already high on something—well, some of them do stupid things." The uniformed officer shrugged. "Well, look around. See if anything's missing."

"Sergeant Macklin?"

A second officer spoke from the doorway, and they all spun about to face him.

"Yeah?" Steve said. "You find something, Somers?"

"Sure did. In the downstairs bathroom, right under the window. He was in a hurry and he dropped this, maybe caught it on the window frame; it's a pretty small space for a grown man to fit through."

He held up a clear plastic bag, and Nick felt his guts twist into a sick knot. A gun, he thought. What if someone in the family had come home while the man was in the house and surprised him?

This kind of thing happened all the time, he thought. To people everywhere. But somehow he'd never expected it to happen in his own home, and he struggled not to let it overwhelm him.

"Run it through ballistics," Steve said. "Maybe we'll get lucky and find he's used it before and we can match it up with something else. Maybe," he added as he and the other two officers left the room, "we'll even get a miracle and pick up a fingerprint or two."

He didn't sound as if he believed that.

Nick drew in a deep breath, listening to their feet clattering down the stairs.

"Shall I help pick things up?" Daisy asked in a small voice. "Or would that make it harder to tell if anything is missing?"

Nick made a snorting sound. His adrenaline level

was high, and he was shaking again, the same as he had when Paul Valerian landed on his car. If he'd caught the guy while he was doing this, he thought, he'd have killed him without even thinking about what the guy could do to *him.*

"What kind of evidence is it going to be if he swiped some of my shorts?" he asked. "Sure. I'd appreciate the help. Wait a minute til I get something to carry stuff in, and I'll pick out what I'm taking with me to Texas."

Daisy, in the act of picking up some of the tapes, stared at him wide eyed. "You're going to Texas? On spring break?"

"Yeah. I'm taking the motorhome, going to see my brother Mickey outside of Houston." Nick swept up a handful of socks and put them on the dresser to take with him. "I'll get a laundry basket for the stuff I want to keep out."

"Don't you have a suitcase? I could loan you a suit—"

"You don't use suitcases in a motorhome. You have drawers and closets. Count me out half a dozen T-shirts, will you, and stick the rest of them back in that drawer."

Daisy complied, placing items carefully into the basket he brought from the bathroom. She was neater than he'd have expected. "Oh," she said suddenly, swooping on some small object, then extending her palm. "It's broken. It was cute."

Nick stared at it. "My dad won that for me when I was about nine. Pitching pennies or something, I forget. I guess it's just cheap junk, but I always liked it." The little figure of a bear was scarcely discernible in the fragments. "Throw it out. It's too smashed to fix."

He dragged the mattress back onto the bed and

threw the covers on it, then began to sort the other stuff.

"When are you leaving?" Daisy asked, subdued.

"Tomorrow night. I'll eat supper at home, probably, and then take off. Drive late, get out of California before daylight. The traffic won't be as bad once I get into Arizona. Here, stick this in there, will you?"

Daisy took the shirt, disapproved of his folding job, and redid it. "I went to Texas once. My sister Marjorie lives in San Antonio. She's married and has this bratty kid Jeremy. I don't suppose you'd like a passenger as far as San Antonio."

"You got that right," Nick agreed.

"Yeah. That's what I thought." Daisy emptied out a drawer and started over again, neatening as she went.

Nick went on restoring order to the room, almost forgetting she was there.

Whoever the jerk was who'd climbed in his window, Nick hoped they caught him and threw him in jail. Of course it didn't seem that he'd taken anything, so probably that meant they wouldn't do much to him even if they did catch him.

He didn't know what was happening in his life lately, but he looked forward with more eagerness than ever to leaving San Sebastian behind, to a few peaceful days with Mickey.

7

Dillinger was at first anxious, then animated with excitement, when he realized that Nick was loading the motorhome. "Yeah, you're going, too. Come on, jump in! Will it make you feel better to be inside, so you're sure I won't leave without you?" Nick asked.

On his third trip carrying groceries, he found Daisy standing outside, peering in through the doorway.

"Boy, this is sure different from the little trailer we took camping last summer! Can I see the inside?"

"Just don't get in my way and slow me down. I expected to do all this last night, but as long as it took to clean up the mess. . . ." His voice trailed away as he led the way inside and began stowing pop cans and frozen dinners in the refrigerator/freezer.

Daisy had eagerly followed him in and was prowling. "Wow! This is neat! A TV and a VCR, a microwave—what's this?"

Nick glanced over his shoulder. "The ice maker. Cold drinks, whenever you want them." He began to empty the carton of cereal and canned goods to go into the cupboards. "As long as you're in here, make yourself useful. See if there's toilet paper in the bathroom, will you? In the space under the sink."

There were more admiring sounds as Daisy checked out the bathroom. "Great shower. That's one reason my mom won't go tent camping anymore, says she can't stand being dirty or taking spit baths. Dad thinks anybody'd have to be crazy to spend this much for an RV, though. I suppose it cost a fortune."

"My dad inherited some money when my grandpa died. He'd always wanted one of these, so Mom told him to go ahead and get it." A lump formed in his throat. "We had a lot of fun in it, the year before he got sick. Was there any toilet paper?"

"Oh, four rolls. What's back there? The bedroom?"

Nick left her poking into every corner and returned to the house for the last load of groceries. His mother smiled at him, adding a big coffee can of cookies to the pile.

"Chocolate chip," she said.

"Thanks, Mom. I think that's about everything. I wonder if I shouldn't just take off now, instead of waiting to have supper at home."

"Steve thinks you'd do better to wait until about seven. For the rush hour traffic to slack off as far as it's going to. You could take a nap for an hour or so, and then you'd be able to drive longer when you get started."

Nick started to object, then fell silent. It was true that traffic would be heavy enough to slow him down for the next couple of hours. Steve had agreed to let him go; maybe he'd better not push his luck.

His mother put a hand on his shoulder—he had grown so tall she had to reach up to it—and spoke softly. "Be careful, Nick. I know you're grown up, and responsible, but I find myself wanting to tell you all those mother-type things: don't drive too fast, don't drive too long at a time, don't pick up hitchhikers. I didn't want to say anything in front of Steve that would give him negative ideas about your traveling alone, but I can't let you go without letting you know how very much your safety means to me. Be careful."

He felt a bit embarrassed. "I will, Mom. I can handle it. And thanks for putting in a good word for me."

She raised onto her toes to kiss him. "Give Mickey my love."

"Yeah, sure, Mom."

She went back to stirring spaghetti sauce on the stove, and Nick wandered toward the front of the house. He wasn't tired, but he remembered that his dad would often take a nap when he expected to be driving late. There wasn't time before supper, though. He decided to see if the paper had come. From what Steve said, the case was closed regarding the death of Paul Valerian, but Nick kept hoping something else would turn up. Something that would help him to understand what had really happened, and why.

The paperboy was just coming, weaving back and forth across the street on his bike, dodging dogs and little kids playing some game on the sidewalk. Nick suddenly came to attention. He hadn't even thought, before, about who the paperboy was.

"Hey, Charlie! Come here a minute, will you?"

Charlie Sparks was a chubby boy with a genial grin.

Nightmare

He rolled to a stop and handed over the newspaper. "Hi, Nick. I heard you got robbed again last night. What's making you such a tempting target?"

"You tell me, and then we'll both know," Nick said, unconsciously echoing a phrase his grandpa had often used. "Listen, Charlie, I wanted to ask you something. The night of the accident, when that guy fell—or jumped, whatever—onto my car, Daisy said you saw some men over there, just before that."

Charlie rolled back and forth a little, rocking the bike. "Yeah. There were three guys up there on the overpass. I saw 'em just before I turned in to the mall. I was going to the show with Teddy Fredricks and Manny Wilkes, and we noticed 'em. I mean, we didn't think anything of it, or anything like that. There were some cars parked down below, and we figured these guys had left 'em there, maybe. Teddy said they were probably making a drug buy, and Manny said, naw, we don't have any big-time dealers in San Sebastian, his dad said so." Manny's father worked in the mayor's office. "We never saw any of 'em before, was the reason we noticed 'em in the first place. That's all."

"Can you remember what they looked like?" Nick pressed.

Charlie jounced up and down again, thinking. "Well, there wasn't anything special about any of 'em. Just ordinary guys, you know."

"Tall? Short? Fat? Skinny?" Nick didn't know why it seemed important to him now, but he couldn't seem to let it drop.

"Medium," Charlie decided.

"All of them?"

"Well, one guy was sort of smaller than the other two, I guess, and skinnier, but none of them was real big or real small. Just ordinary."

"Do you remember what they were wearing?"

"Jackets, I guess. Not shirtsleeves, anyway. It was kind of cool that night. One of 'em had glasses. I think that was the smallest one. I saw the light reflecting off the glasses when he turned his head. You think they had something to do with the guy that fell?"

"Did any of them look like the guy that fell? Were you in the crowd, afterward? Did you get a look at him, that Paul Valerian?"

Charlie stopped rolling back and forth. "Well, I was there. We all came over. Missed the first half hour of the movie and then my dad came looking for me because we stayed later to catch the beginning. Anyway, I saw the guy on the road. But I couldn't tell you what he looked like, you know. Just a pile of clothes. Teddy was closer. He said there was blood on the pavement after they picked him up and took him away."

Nick struggled with frustration. "But he *could* have been one of the three guys you saw a few minutes earlier?"

"Yeah, I guess so. He *could* have been."

So what did that prove, even if it were true? Nick didn't know, but he felt the compulsion to keep digging at it, even if he didn't exactly know why. He took another tack. "What about the cars you saw? Did you pay any real attention? Do you know what they were?"

Charlie was more certain and more exact about the cars. "Red Camero, an old brown Chevy Malibu—about a '78, I think, my uncle had one like it—and a dark blue T-Bird, fairly new."

Nightmare

If the cars were significant, Nick didn't have any way of knowing how. He went back to the men on the overpass. "Did the guys seem to be arguing? Having a friendly discussion? What?"

Charlie shrugged. "I don't know. They were just standing there talking, was all *I* saw. Nobody was waving their arms around or acting hostile or anything. Why?" Curiosity finally struck him. "You think the other two threw him over the edge or something?"

"I don't know. The police say he jumped. The case is closed. Did you notice if the cars were still there after the guy fell?"

Charlie shook his head. "Nope. I never paid any attention if they were still there. All the cop cars, and the ambulance, and all the people—man, it was a mess. I never looked toward the cars. Hey, listen, I got to deliver the rest of my papers. Old man Samuels gets nasty if I'm late with his. I'll see you, Nick."

Nick walked back inside, carrying the paper, dropping it on Steve's recliner. The one way he could think of that Steve was like his dad was that they both insisted on reading a virgin paper, neither folded nor clipped by anyone else before they were finished with it.

Another couple of hours, he thought, and he'd be on the road. Away from Steve, away from his sometimes overanxious mother, away from dorky Daisy and burglars trashing his room and the possibility of meeting Lisa on the street.

He couldn't wait to get started.

Even though he waited until seven o'clock before he pulled out of the yard, Dillinger acting very pleased to be accompanying him in the passenger seat, the first hour or so of driving was pretty slow. Rush hour came early and lasted late on California freeways.

Nick didn't feel pressured, though. To his relief he felt no nervousness about driving the big motorhome. It was thirty feet long and eight feet wide, and that intimidated his mother, but it handled beautifully. Besides that, it was big enough so people saw you coming and maybe a few of them thought twice before cutting in front of you, though there were always a few idiots who didn't.

He was aware of going under the first couple of overpasses (they all had wire-mesh guards to prevent rocks or bodies from being dropped onto cars below) and then they didn't intrude on his consciousness anymore.

Dillinger was a good companion. He minded well, stayed in his seat, and was an excellent listener. Nick had always thought the dog was his best excuse for talking to himself, for thinking aloud. Dillinger was never critical and never bored.

They pulled onto Old 99, southbound, and Nick let the speed climb to the legal limit and put the coach on cruise control. "Too bad you don't know how to open the refrigerator," he told the dog. "You could get me a cold Pepsi."

Dillinger, ears pricked up, eyes bright, tried to wag the tail he was sitting on, eager to understand. Nick was grateful for his presence.

He liked driving. He was glad Steve had made him drive again right away, or he might not have been able to do this. Nick felt better than he had in weeks, months.

Nightmare

He felt free of school—he'd retaken the calculus test and knew he had at least a passing grade this time—and memories of Lisa, and the friction at home. He wouldn't even have dorky Daisy watching his bedroom window or intercepting him every time he left the house or returned to it.

Actually, he thought, able to grin now that he had cut loose from all that, Daisy wasn't so bad, for a kid. Lots of kids were pests. She'd probably be OK when she grew up.

The day faded, and the lights came on. Fresno, Tulare, Delano. At Bakersfield he caught Highway 58, heading first east, then south, handling the motorhome easily, fairly relaxed. By this time Dillinger had tired of looking out the windows and curled in the seat, taking a snooze.

Nick felt wide awake, intending to go as far as he could before he stopped to sleep. Into Arizona, anyway. If he could, he'd go all the way across the desert before it got hot, but the distance was too far to do it all tonight. The coach had air-conditioning, so even if it got warm they'd be comfortable. This early in the year it shouldn't be too bad, anyway.

At Palmdale he cut across 138 toward San Bernardino and the connection with Interstate 10, which would take him all the way into Texas. "Piece of cake," he'd told Dillinger when he was plotting it out on the map.

He stopped at a rest stop amid all the eighteen wheelers, long enough to relieve himself and get a can of Pepsi and make a thick ham and cheese sandwich. He ate one of the oranges he'd brought; he didn't have many because he knew the authorities were unlikely to allow him to take fresh fruit into Arizona. They were even fussier than California border inspectors about the possibility of transferring fruit flies or other destructive insects or diseases, so he planned to buy fruit after he'd crossed the border.

There weren't as many lights now as he went on. Small towns: Banning, Palm Springs, Indio. And then a long stretch with virtually nothing to watch except the big trucks that ran all night long. Larry's dad owned a small trucking firm, and Larry intended to drive for him when he got out of school, though his folks were holding out for a college education before he eventually took over the business. Nick thought he might enjoy driving for a living, at least for a while. He wondered if Larry's dad might hire him through the summer, so he could build up a cash reserve for college. He'd be eighteen in June.

He listened to the chatter on the CB. His dad had always kept it on when they were on the freeways; he said it helped to know ahead of time when there were accidents or road hazards he'd have to contend with. Someone came on wanting to know how the road looked to the east. "Any Smokeys behind you west bounders?" he asked, meaning officers of the California Highway Patrol.

Nick chuckled at the response. "Roll up your windows and lock your doors," a second driver suggested. "There's nobody out there to protect you between here and Buckeye."

That, naturally, was another function of the CBs. The truckers kept one another apprised of the location of the troopers who patrolled the freeways. And called for help when it was needed.

Nightmare

Nick crossed the border at Blythe—went through the inspection station where they checked out his refrigerator for contraband fruit—and decided it was time to call a halt. He was, quite suddenly, dead tired.

Dillinger roused from his nap and stretched as the coach rolled to a halt in a rest stop.

"OK, Dill, we'll walk around the rig, check the tires and the oil, and give you a breather. Wait'll I get the leash," Nick told him as he set the brakes.

He was hungry again when they reentered the coach, and this time he stuck a Mexican dinner in the microwave and ate it, opening a can of dog food for Dillinger.

By the time he was ready for sleep, he was suddenly staggering with fatigue. It was all catching up with him.

He was peeling off his T-shirt as he entered the rear bedroom and flicked the light switch.

Dillinger gave a delighted yip and leaped onto the right-hand bunk, and Nick stopped short in consternation.

"What the hell are you doing here?" he demanded furiously.

8

Daisy rolled over and sat up, blinking under the overhead light. "Oh, hi, Nick. Where are we?"

Nick almost choked in his rage and dismay. "We're in Arizona. I just transported an underage girl across a state line! I think they hang a guy for that!"

She ran a hand through tousled coppery curls, squinting up at him. "Doesn't it have to be for immoral purposes for them to do that?"

"This isn't funny, Daisy! You idiot, how could you have been so *stupid*! We've probably had every CHP officer in California trying to intercept us before we got out of the state, and by now they'll have alerted the state police here!"

"Oh, don't be silly. My folks don't even know I'm gone yet." Daisy yawned and absently patted Dillinger, beside her on the bed. "When they find out in the morning, they'll think I'm on a bus on my way to Marjorie's in San Antonio. I left a note."

It was all Nick could do to keep from hitting her.

Nightmare

"How *dared* you do this to me? You had no right, Daisy! I ought to kill you!"

Dillinger licked her chin, and she put an arm around him. "I only want a ride to my sister's. Remember, I told you Marjorie lives in San Antonio? I brought some of my own groceries and I have some money, so I won't cost you anything."

Nick practically snarled. "It isn't the money, you moron! Your folks will send the cops after us, and then where will I be?"

"I could always tell the truth," Daisy pointed out. "Tell everybody I stowed away, that you didn't know I was here. Only I won't have to, because they think I got on a bus. Or they will, when they read my note. I told them I couldn't stand Aunt Wilma for another week and a half, and Marjorie wanted me to come and visit and said she'd pay my bus fare, so I took the money out of my savings account."

"And what happens when they call your sister to see if you got there all right?" Nick asked. "And she says she hasn't heard from you in two months?"

"She won't. She'll cover for me until I get there. We've always covered for each other. She'll tell them I'm in the shower or gone to a drug store or something so I can't come to the phone. Marjorie's neat, Nick. You'll like her."

"Not if she's anything like you," Nick retorted, grinding his teeth. "What am I going to do with you now? If I take you back home I'll lose a couple of days, and I won't even have time to get to see Mickey! *Damn* you anyway, Daisy!"

"Don't take me home. That would be stupid. Just

take me on to my sister's. They all think I'm on a bus and they'll never know the difference. Come on, Nick. You miss your brother, and I miss my sister. What's the difference?"

"The difference is that my folks know where I am, and I didn't stow away in somebody else's motorhome."

Nick smacked a palm against the wall, trying to think what to do next. He was dead tired. He'd been driving half the night, and he knew that although adrenaline was buoying him up right now, he'd never be able to drive after it had worn off. He'd have to sleep for a while before he could turn around and take her home. And then, he realized in deep frustration, he'd have to sleep again before he retraced his way back to here.

He didn't have time. Not if he was going to spend a few days with Mickey and get back to school after the break.

"You look beat," Daisy said with what seemed genuine concern. "Get some rest, think about it. You'll see I'm right. You're going through San Antonio anyway, aren't you? So what's the big deal? Just leave me off at my sister's and go on. I'll take the bus back if you don't want to pick me up when you leave Houston—"

"I *don't* want to pick you up at any time!"

"—so it will all work out. Come on, Nick. Be a good sport."

"This has nothing to do with being a good sport. This isn't a game; it could have serious consequences, can't you see that?"

"But it won't if nobody knows about it. Marjorie will be the only one, and she won't tell. She never tells on me."

Nightmare

Nick's shoulders sagged in temporary defeat. He was so bushed he was swaying on his feet, and his head wasn't working too well, either.

"If I still feel the way I do now when I wake up," he told her ominously, "I'm going to kill you."

"Okay. Listen, can I use the bathroom now? I didn't dare while you were driving for fear you'd see me, or Dillinger would get excited and tip you off. He did come sniffing back by the bedroom door when you first got in, but you called him off and told him to get into his seat. I got out of bed once, when you were stopped back there and walked Dill outside for a minute, but I was so scared you'd come back I didn't dare take long—"

He stared at her, wondering what it would take to get through to her the enormity of what she had done. "Go. But if you think I'm going to sleep on the couch up front and give you the bedroom, you're crazy. You can sleep out there yourself."

Daisy paused in the act of pushing past him into the narrow passageway toward the bathroom. "The other bunk is fine. What's the big deal? Neither one of us is undressed, anyway."

"I'm *getting* undressed," Nick told her. "So if you don't want to see me in my shorts, stay in the bathroom for five minutes. And don't run a lot of water. We're not hooked up to a supply, so all there is is what's in the tank."

"OK." She sounded so offhand that he wanted to smack her as she went past. She'd probably be offhand about that, too.

Nick stripped to his shorts and climbed into the other bunk. He'd slept in it many times in the past, but he'd never had a trip like this one.

He didn't know what he ought to do. Call Daisy's folks and tell them where she was and the circumstances of the matter? He didn't know the McCallums except to speak to in passing. Her mother was dark and thin and intense looking. Her voice was often cross when she called Daisy. Mr. McCallum was heavyset and tough looking—he was a plumber—and the source of Daisy's red hair, only his was darker and going bald. He didn't look like a man who would appreciate hearing that his younger daughter was on a trip in a motorhome with the boy next door.

Jeeze, what a mess! The idea of talking to Daisy's dad turned him off completely. Would Mr. McCallum, or anyone, believe he hadn't known about Daisy?

What, then? Nick stared up at the ceiling. Put her on a bus, he thought. Even if he had to come up with part of the fare himself, if she didn't have enough money, and ship her back to San Sebastian. Wash his hands of her.

Yeah, that's what he'd do. Stop at the next place they could get a bus and send her home.

God, he was tired. He closed his eyes, only to open them a minute later when he heard Daisy returning. She was wearing pink pajamas with teddy bears on them. He stared at her, his mouth dropping open.

Daisy turned on the small lamp at the head of her bed, then flicked the switch to extinguish the overhead fixture. She saw him watching her. "Don't say it. My grandma still thinks I'm six years old. She gave me the pajamas for my birthday."

"She knows your mental age, anyway," Nick said, unable to suppress the savage note in his voice. "Nobody would take you for an adult, that's for sure. Not with the stupid things you keep doing."

"What's stupid about wanting to see my sister? I miss her. And I *hate* having Aunt Wilma in my room and having to eat all that yucky stuff she insists on. This is a good time to visit Marjorie. I'll go home when Aunt Wilma's gone."

She turned back the spread and got into bed. "Boy, this is a neat way to travel."

She turned off the lamp, leaving them in darkness except for the light that seeped in through the blinds from the parking area outside. Beside them a refrigerator truck with its generator running only emphasized the stillness inside their own coach.

Nick debated whether it would be worth the effort to get out of bed and strangle her or if he should wait until morning.

He was asleep before he made up his mind.

And then the dreams began again. The nightmare, only with variations that were no improvement over the original one, of the man sliding into his windshield, of watching the glass splinter and crack and turn opaque, so that the terrified face finally disappeared.

"Nick! For pete's sake, Nick, wake up! What're you dreaming?"

He came awake instantly, shuddering, gasping, drenched in sweat.

It wasn't only the dream, which was already receding into a jumbled, confused montage of threatening men and a figure hurtling off an overpass and Mr.

McCallum slamming him up against a wall and punching his face in.

"God, it's hot in here! I feel like I'm suffocating!"

"Yeah. I tried opening a window, but with trucks on both side of us with their motors running I couldn't stand the fumes. Besides, we need cross ventilation, and I wasn't sure I could get your window open without waking you up. And then you started threshing around and crying."

"I wasn't crying," Nick said automatically, though he was not absolutely certain of that. "I was having nightmares again."

"You do that all the time?" Daisy, who had been hovering over him, sank back on the opposite bunk. He could barely see her in the dimness.

"Ever since the accident." Nick threw off what was left of his covers and stood up. "I'm going to turn the generator on and run the air conditioner. And I need something to drink."

"Me, too," Daisy agreed at once. "I didn't dare drink much while I was hiding for fear I'd have to come out to the bathroom. Can I have a can of your pop? I brought some, but I didn't dare put it in the refrigerator, so mine's warm."

Nick groped his way out of the bedroom to the control panel where he hit the switch for the generator. It came on instantly with a low hum. A moment later the air conditioner kicked in, and he knew the temperature would begin to drop almost immediately.

In the meantime, he'd quench his thirst. He didn't want to turn on one of the overhead lights, but it didn't matter. He knew where he'd put the pop. He found two cans—anything wet would do—and padded back to the bedroom with them, thrusting one at Daisy.

"No ice?" she asked, accepting the frosty can.

"You're pushing your luck," Nick warned her. "It wouldn't take much to make me shove you out the door right here in the rest area. Get your own ice if you want it."

"Oh, I guess this is good and cold." She took a long sip. "Mmm. That hits the spot."

"I'd like to hit the spot. Right between your eyes."

Daisy sipped again before she answered. "Are you always this crabby when you wake up?"

"Crabby?" Nick echoed, incredulous. "Just because you stowed away, after lying to your folks, who'll probably kill me when they find out where you are, and setting me up so if the cops stop us for anything they'll throw me in jail forever for transporting a female minor across a state line? You don't think that ought to make me crabby?"

Outflanked, Daisy changed the subject. "What were you dreaming about? You scared me."

"It scared me, too. I haven't had nightmares like this since Mickey convinced me there was a dragon under my bed, when I was four." Nick drained his pop can and put it on the nightstand between their beds. "What time you got?"

Daisy leaned back, making a space between the venetian blinds so that enough light would shine through to illuminate her watch. "A quarter after four."

Nick groaned. "I need more sleep than this before I can keep going."

Daisy was still looking through the opening in the blinds. "Some guy next to us is sleeping in his car. I bet he's uncomfortable compared to us. That air conditioner works great, doesn't it? It covers up the sounds of those darned trucks, too."

Nick scowled. "There's a car next to us? Cars are supposed to park on the other side and leave this area for bigger rigs. There are always a few jerks who don't care, though, if they keep somebody else from having a big enough parking spot."

"Like the people who park in spaces for the hand-icapped," Daisy agreed, letting the shades fall back into place. "They don't care about the other guy, as long as they get what they want."

"Like you didn't think about what a predicament you were putting me in by stowing away."

"You're not in any trouble unless somebody finds out, and why would they? My folks trust me. If I said I went to Marjorie's, they'll believe it."

"Shows how smart *they* are," Nick muttered un-graciously. "I'm going back to sleep. The quicker I get rested enough to drive, the quicker I can get rid of you."

Daisy didn't seem to take offense at anything he said, which was exasperating in itself. "OK. Do you want me to wake you up again if you have another nightmare?"

"Don't do me any favors," Nick told her. And then when there was no reaction from her, and he remem-bered how bad the dreams could be, he added gruffly, "Yeah. If I start yelling or anything, wake me up."

Daisy didn't answer, and he thought maybe she'd already dozed off again.

The air temperature was considerably improved now, and he drew the sheet over himself and closed his eyes, hoping that for the rest of the night, at least, the nightmares were over.

9

Nick woke feeling chilled, for the air conditioner still hummed overhead. The other bunk was empty, neatly made up. Maybe, he thought hopefully, it had all been one of the nightmares; Daisy hadn't been there at all.

And then, immediately, he realized he smelled bacon and toast.

No nightmare. It was real, and Daisy was fixing breakfast.

He wasn't going to take her home, he'd already decided that. To do so would mean aborting the whole trip, and he wanted more urgently than ever to see Mickey. Somehow he was convinced that if he talked it all over with his brother he'd be better able to handle everything: the accident, the situation at home with his stepfather, the sense of violation that came from having had his room ransacked and trashed.

So he'd put Daisy on a bus at the first place it was possible. She wasn't his responsibility, after all.

He got up and pulled on jeans and a shirt, jerking the covers into place and turning off the air conditioner before he left the bedroom.

Daisy, a coppery tendril falling across her forehead, turned from the stove. "Hi. You didn't have any more nightmares."

"No. What time is it?"

"Quarter after eight. Boy, those trucks are sure noisy! They kept waking me up. Traveling by motorhome is great, but it's too bad they don't have better places to park them than next to twenty big rigs that don't shut their motors off."

She dropped two more slices of bread into the toaster and buttered the two she had just taken out.

"They do," Nick said, heading for the bathroom.

"Do what?" Her eyes, up close, were green and wide.

"Do have better places to park, where there aren't any trucks. They have RV parks, where you can plug into shore power and water, and drain your tanks. Only you usually have to get off the freeway to find one, and they charge you money. It's cheaper and easier to use a rest stop most of the time."

He went into the bathroom and closed the door.

They ate in the sunny dinette—bacon, eggs, toast, and Pepsi. "How come you didn't bring any juice?" Daisy wanted to know.

"What are you, my mother?" Nick asked, but without rancor. It was more bearable having her around now that he knew he was getting rid of her soon. At least she knew how to wash dishes.

"It's interesting, watching people," Daisy said as a family with young children and a dog spilled out of a car and headed toward the rest rooms. "There's a lady with three poodles over there; they all had their leashes tangled around her when I took Dillinger out."

"I hope you took him over to the pet area, instead of letting him do his business on the grass where those kids are," Nick said, feeling better now that his stomach was filled. "Listen, you might as well know right now what I'm going to do. In the next town we'll find a bus station, and you're getting on a bus, going home."

Daisy's face was suddenly stricken. "Nick! What a crummy idea!"

"The crummy idea," Nick corrected her, "was you stowing away in my motorhome. I'm not kidding, Daisy, it was way out of line. You could get me arrested and thrown in jail, and don't go over the same arguments you used last night about it won't matter if nobody knows. Somebody *could* know. Your dad would kill me, *my* folks would kill me, if they knew I took you out of California. So you figure on packing your pink teddy bear pajamas and being ready for the bus in the next half hour or so."

"Aw, come on, Nick! It's not that far to San Antonio—"

"Only across two more state lines," Nick said.

"—and I'll stay out of sight, if that's what you want. Only take me to Marjorie's—"

"I'm putting you on a bus," Nick told her flatly, "and you're going home."

A stubborn look came over her face. "You can't make me go home. If I have to get on a bus, I'll head on to San Antonio."

"Fine. As long as you get out of my coach and nobody can hold me responsible."

Her face crumpled. "Nick, please! I haven't really got enough money to take the bus and still have enough to get home."

"You said your sister would pay for it, didn't you?"

"Well, she would, if she could afford it, but maybe she can't. She's always broke. She borrows money from my folks sometimes."

Nick hardened his heart. "Tough. You should have thought of all this before you came up with the crazy idea of stowing away on me. Clean up in here, will you, while I check the outside and make sure everything is OK."

When he came back, the small kitchen was spotless and his passenger seemed resigned, if not happily so. She belted herself into the copilot's seat, with an ecstatic Dillinger on her lap, and Nick waited for a truck and trailer to pull out before he took his turn.

"That jerk in the car is still here," he observed, glancing in his mirror. "It always amazes me how many people can't read signs—or decide they only apply to someone else."

Daisy said nothing. He hoped she wasn't going to cry. Not that it would make him change his mind, but he had trouble handling it when a girl cried.

It was bright and sunny as they headed east on Interstate 10 toward Phoenix. It was a long stretch across the desert, with not much to be seen. Traffic, as always, was heavy, but the road was straight and flat and Nick put it on cruise control again.

"Doesn't look as if there will be many bus stations out here," Daisy said finally, after twenty minutes of total silence.

"Oh, don't worry. Some of these little crossroads places have bus stops," Nick assured her. "There, see that sign? For the Indian jewelry and souvenirs? It's a bus stop, too."

Daisy's shoulder's slumped and she muttered something under her breath; it was probably just as well that he couldn't make out what it was.

There must have been a dozen signs advertising the place before they came to the little cluster of buildings that included a tourist-trap store, a restaurant, and a gas station. Nick eased the motorhome into the parking lot and shut it down. This time of day there were only a few cars and a handful of tourists.

"Come on. I'll go with you and see you get your ticket."

"Not back to San Sebastian," Daisy insisted. "I'm going to San Antonio."

"Suit yourself. Just as long as you don't go with me."

They descended from the coach, with its tinted windows, and stood blinking in the glare of the sun. An older couple, loaded with packages, came out of the restaurant, laughing and talking.

Nick closed the door so that a protesting Dillinger couldn't join them and then touched Daisy's elbow. "Over there," he said.

It wasn't really a bus station, only a sign over the cashier's counter at the end of the restaurant where several truckers and a small family were having breakfast. The girl behind the register responded to Nick's query without consulting a schedule.

"San Antonio? Sure. Next bus is in about two hours.

Eleven-twenty. I'll be with you in a minute."

A man detached himself from the nearest wall and leaned toward them. "Going on the bus?" he asked Daisy.

She drew back, bumping into Nick, not answering.

"Going to El Paso, myself," the man said. He was young but scruffy looking, his eyes suggesting that he was high on something. "Be glad to help with your luggage. Or whatever."

"She doesn't need your help," Nick said sharply.

"Yeah? Let her speak for herself, eh? I saw you drivin' that fancy motorhome, *you* ain't goin' on no bus, are you? Maybe the little lady's got other ideas. Maybe she'd like company."

"No," Daisy said, finding her tongue. "I don't need any company." She turned away from him, but the man was persistent.

"I'm good company," he insisted. "Hey, Ralph, ain't I good company?"

Another man, who looked even scruffier, had emerged from the men's room, still adjusting his clothes. He was wearing a leather jacket and working a toothpick around in his mouth.

"Sure, man," he agreed, his gaze moving over Daisy's slight figure. "We're both good company. You going to El Paso, too? How about we all go together?"

Daisy lifted frightened eyes to Nick. "Not from here," she said in a pleading tone. "Not on this bus."

Nick's hesitation was brief. He couldn't very well abandon her to wait here for two hours with these two stoned creeps pestering her, and it didn't make sense to lose two hours waiting with her.

"Come on," he said, and knew by the derisive and

suggestive remarks that followed them that he'd made the only possible decision.

Daisy was already recovering as they emerged once more into the morning sunshine. "Sheesh, what a couple of jerks," she said.

"Yeah. Only you are taking the bus, from somewhere farther down the road," Nick said.

Daisy glanced across the parking area to where a dark blue sedan was pulling into a space. "There's the guy from the rest stop. Maybe he's going to San Antonio," she said blithely. "Maybe I could ask him for a ride."

Nick looked to see if she was serious. "Your brain must be about as big as a pea. Or maybe the head of a pin."

"Don't be so stuffy. I'm only kidding. I know how stupid it is to hitchhike. Gosh, I bet it's going to get hot today. It must be eighty degrees already, and it's only a little after nine o'clock."

Nick hesitated uncertainly, looking at the motorhome. "I don't really need gas yet—that thing will run over 600 miles on a tank—but the way things are going, maybe I'd better top it off while we have a chance." He headed toward an attendant to tell him to fill it up.

Dillinger welcomed them back with enthusiasm, and they took off again. Daisy was silent for the first few miles, and when she spoke she'd reverted to the mood induced by the men in the restaurant behind them.

"You know, even if I catch the bus on down the road, those guys are going to be on it."

He hadn't thought of that, but she had a point, though he hated to admit it.

"They scared me."

Still Nick didn't say anything.

"You'd never forgive yourself if anything happened to me." Daisy shot him a sideways glance. "Imagine, if they found my broken and mutilated body alongside the road. Remember that girl who was attacked and had her arms chopped off before the guy threw her out of his car? He thought she was dead, but she lived and identified him. They let him out of prison but no town would agree that he could go and live in their community—"

"I read the papers," Nick said. "I remember it."

"It was terrible what happened to her."

"She was hitchhiking, if I remember right," Nick said.

"Yeah, but even traveling on a bus, you have to get off sometimes, right? For meals, rest stops. And I'd probably have a bus change in El Paso, right? I might have to hang around the bus station for a couple of hours, with characters like those two around, waiting for a connecting bus to San Antonio. Maybe that's why my dad didn't want me to travel by bus."

"You talked to him about it? And he didn't want you to go?"

Daisy shrugged. "He objects to everything I want to do, just the way he did with Marjorie. Mom sometimes helps me talk him around, but she didn't want me to go to my sister's on the bus, either, and I couldn't afford to fly. Nick, listen. It'll only take a couple of days to get to San Antonio, right? What harm will it do if I stay with you? I won't cause any trouble. And I'll be safe. You won't have to worry about me."

"Who says I'm worrying about you?" Nick asked rudely. But he was. He hadn't encouraged her to come, would have refused if he'd discovered her before they were so far from home, but in a way he supposed she was his responsibility now.

She was right about those guys being on the bus. Even if Daisy sat right behind the driver—which might not be possible—there was no guarantee that the driver could protect her from a couple of creeps determined to harass her.

Any other girl would have been put down by his attitude. Daisy kept right on talking. "It's always been easy for me to imagine being people like that. The girl who got her arms cut off, I mean. I think about what she must have gone through, before he left her for dead. Did he cut her up with a knife before he chopped off her arms?"

"Knock it off!" Nick exploded. "Just shut up, OK?"

"But don't you do that? Imagine yourself having that kind of experience, when you read about it?"

"I've been having plenty of experiences of my own lately," Nick told her, tight lipped. "I don't need to imagine anything extra."

She subsided then, looking out the window at the passing landscape, dry and barren of vegetation except for an occasional clump of some early spring flowers, tiny orange ones in sprays no more than a foot and a half high.

She looked at him but didn't say anything when the coach rolled on past another tourist spot, this one looking busier, with a sign indicating it was a bus stop.

When he didn't slow at the following one, either, Daisy smiled. "You won't be sorry, Nick," she told him.

She relaxed after that, and he had to admit that when she wasn't imagining being the victim of an intended hatchet murderer, Daisy wasn't bad company. She saved him stopping time, too. She got up to get him a cold drink when he wanted it, and made peanut butter sandwiches, which they ate while they kept on moving.

He knew better than to drive too long at a time without rest, though. His dad had always stopped every two hours, at least long enough to walk around the vehicle and check tires, to give himself a change of position, to have something to eat or drink.

At their second rest stop, Daisy decided it was time for lunch.

"How about if I heat up a couple of those chicken dinners? Can I use the microwave?"

"Sure. I have to run the generator for it to work," Nick said, reaching for the switch. He'd have to figure on replenishing his supplies, he thought resignedly. Daisy's contribution to the food consisted mostly of junk. Except, he discovered when she brought them out, a few oranges.

He stared at them in dismay. "It's illegal to smuggle fruit into Arizona. If they'd found them when they stopped us at the border inspection station—especially after I told them I didn't have any fruit with me—for pete's sake, Daisy, I can't believe you!"

"Well, I didn't know they were illegal when I put them in my bag. And now we're eating them, so they aren't going to contaminate anything, are they? Besides, I'm pretty sure these came from Arizona in the first place. I already peeled them, so there's no sense wasting them, is there? How long before we get to Phoenix?"

He knew she was changing the subject, but he let her do it. Boy, would he be glad to turn her over to her sister in San Antonio before she pulled any more surprises.

The next one, though, was hardly Daisy's fault. She had gotten out of the coach to carry a plastic bag of trash to one of the garbage containers in the rest stop, and she came back looking thoughtful.

"That guy pulled in here, too. The guy in the dark blue car, the one who used up a truck space last night at the rest stop."

"There's only one main road," Nick said, checking the gauges before they moved on. "And only a few places to stop. Everybody going from California to Arizona, New Mexico, or Texas is using the same ones."

"Yeah, I guess," Daisy agreed. But after they'd gone through Phoenix at midday and swung southeast toward Tucson, she moved uneasily in her seat, eyes fixed on the big outside mirror as they rounded a curve. "You know something, Nick? I think that guy is following us."

"Who? What guy?"

"The one in the dark blue sedan, the one that parked along side of us last night, where he didn't belong."

Uneasiness prickled along Nick's spine, though it didn't show in his voice. He was remembering Charlie Sparks's description of those cars that had been parked near the overpass when Paul Valerian died.

"What kind of car is it? A Thunderbird? Can you tell?"

"I'm not real good on cars," Daisy confessed. "New-ish looking, nice car. That's all I know. Why don't you slow down, see if he'll pass you."

To his own surprise, Nick did as she'd suggested.

"Nope." Daisy reported what he could tell for himself. "He's slowing down, too. Why would he be following us?"

"I don't know," Nick said slowly, "but maybe I ought to see if you're right. I'm going off at the first exit, then circle back onto the freeway without stopping. Help me keep an eye on him."

When the exit sign came up, Nick flipped on his right turn signal and took the curve at the required lower speed limit.

Daisy sounded breathless, and her green eyes were wide. "He's right behind us," she said.

10

"**W**hy?" Daisy asked, sounding a bit breathless. "Why is he following us?"

Nick was already swinging the big coach back onto the freeway approach, returning to the mainstream of traffic. His heart was thudding audibly, though he remained surface calm. "Good question. The only thing that occurs to me is based on what Charlie Sparks told me." He watched the mirrors and caught a glimpse of the dark blue sedan behind him. He'd been seeing it, off and on, ever since they started out that morning, and it had seemed no more than just another fellow traveler. Now it was suddenly ominous.

"Charlie? What's he got to do with anything?" Daisy was watching the mirrors, too.

"He couldn't do a good job of describing the three men he saw on the overpass just before Paul Valerian went over the railing, but he remembered the cars. You know Charlie, his uncle has the junkyard, and Charlie and his dad get to rob old cars for parts for theirs. He knows cars pretty well."

Daisy moistened her lips, her attention still fixed on the car behind them. "He's dropped back, but he's right behind us."

"Charlie said one of the cars was a fairly new Thunderbird. That's what *that* one is, and I'm trying to figure out the connection, if there is one." And then, more to reassure them both than from conviction, he added, "It could just be a coincidence, of course. There are probably a million dark blue T-Birds."

"Sure," Daisy agreed. "And he just happened to want to swing off the freeway just now, and right back onto it without stopping anywhere, the way we did."

"I should have stopped somewhere," Nick said. "In an area where it's unlikely an ordinary traveler would have stopped. To see if he kept an eye on us there, too. Now we've tipped him off that we're on to him."

"Maybe not. Take this next off-ramp," Daisy said, "and go into a service station or something; act like we took the wrong exit by mistake. That might throw him off. He can't know *for sure* that we noticed him."

Nick flipped the turn signal and followed her suggestion, pulling into a Shell station but not stopping at the pumps. "I'll go inside, ask a question or something, pretend I don't notice the guy in the T-Bird. Keep an eye on him. Try to see what he looks like if he follows us in."

He felt really strange, leaving the coach and walking across the macadam without looking back. He'd always enjoyed movies of intrigue and danger, but he wasn't enjoying this much.

The compulsion to look over his shoulder when he heard a car behind him was overwhelming, but Nick resisted the urge and entered the station. The car rolled past him, to the forward pumps, and he saw to his relief that it was a white Corolla.

"Yessir, what can I do for you?" the attendant asked.

It was a phenomenon Joe Corelli had noticed as soon as he got the motorhome. Anyone driving one was likely to be addressed as "sir," even a driver as young as Nick, or an older one in faded jeans. Instant prestige, Joe had called it, laughing.

God, Nick thought, he wished his dad were here, that they were on their way to a week in the High Sierra, an innocent and carefree excursion with nothing to think about but enjoying themselves.

"Sir?" the man repeated, and Nick said the first thing that occurred to him.

"I need a new water hose, thought I'd see if you have one that would fit my coach."

"We got a few if you want to look. What do you need?"

While the man was showing him the supply, Nick glanced out the window. There was no sign of the blue T-Bird. Had they been mistaken? Did its driver have no interest in them after all?

"This one will work," Nick said, reaching out blindly for the first hose that came to hand.

He carried it prominently displayed as he strode back out to the coach, in case anyone was interested in why he had stopped. Daisy met him in the doorway.

"He's on the other side of the road, in front of that little fast-food place."

Nick's heart skipped a beat. "Did you get a look at him?"

"No. He didn't get out of the car. Hasn't done a thing except sit there."

Nick cursed with feeling. "So we still don't know for sure he knows we're on to him, but it sure looks as if he *is* following us. I don't think he's a pro, though. I mean, not a cop or a private detective, anything like that."

Daisy moved out of his way so he could maneuver to look out the window, across the road. Sure enough, there was the dark blue car.

"Can't see the license plates. I wonder if they're from California? Listen, when I pull out of here I'm going to swing past him, as close as I can get. See if you can get a good look at his plates, OK? Or the driver himself. I don't suppose you saw him when he was parked beside us?"

"Just a guy sleeping. I never saw his face. Nick, do you think it has something to do with that Valerian guy?"

"If it does, Valerian didn't jump from that overpass," Nick said, moving back to the driver's seat. "I never believed he did, and I'm getting surer of that by the minute." He buckled in and started the motor.

"You think he was murdered," Daisy said, taking her own seat, her fingers suddenly clumsy with the seat belt. "Don't you?"

Nick didn't answer. He didn't *want* to think anything of the sort, though in a way that truth could release *him* from a terrible sense of responsibility. But the implications of *murder* boggled his mind. Especially if there was a connection between *that* and the fact that a car that matched the description of one on the scene when the fall took place appeared to be following them now.

Nightmare

Daisy dug into her purse for a pencil and an address book, holding them ready as Nick pulled out, crossed the road, and made a turn through the parking lot of the fast-food place.

"The windows are tinted too dark and the sun's reflecting off the glass; I couldn't see a thing inside," Daisy informed him as they eased past the other vehicle. "I got the license plate number, though. It's from California. An Alameda dealer's plate holder."

Nick grunted, heading toward the on-ramp to I-10 East. He'd only been this way once before, and he didn't really remember much about it, but once away from the cities there was no likelihood of getting lost. The freeway was straight and flat, and there was little to confuse even the most inexperienced driver.

It was several minutes before Daisy spoke in a subdued voice. "Why is he following us, Nick?"

"Your guess is as good as mine." He swung around a slow-moving pickup loaded with chicken crates. "Maybe I ought to stop and ask him."

She gave a startled look. "But if he's a murderer . . . what if he is? What if he wants to murder *us*?"

"He's had at least one chance to do that. He slept in a car right beside us all last night. We weren't even suspicious then."

Daisy shivered. "What are we going to do?"

"I don't know," Nick said, staring straight ahead.

He needed Mickey more than he had at any time since their dad had died, and Mickey was almost twelve hundred miles away, with most of three states between them. Even if he stopped and called him, what could Mickey do? What advice could he offer?

He could call Steve. The thought slipped into his mind unbidden. Steve was a cop. He would know what to do.

"I guess Steve would tell me to find the nearest police station and tell them everything I know, or suspect," he said aloud. "Only how much attention are they going to pay to a seventeen-year-old kid driving an expensive motorhome, which they're going to question, when the cops back home decided Paul Valerian was a suicide and the guy in the blue Thunderbird hasn't done anything except use the same highway and pull off at the same time we have. And they'd also want to know why I was carrying a fifteen-year-old kid—a *female* kid whose parents don't know where she is—across all these state lines."

"So it's no cops, huh?" Daisy asked in a small voice.

"Not unless the guy does something more than drive behind us and pull off the freeway at the same time we do," Nick said grimly.

There was no more mention of putting Daisy on a bus, either back to San Sebastian or on to San Antonio. If Nick was in danger—which they couldn't say for sure—then keeping Daisy with him put *her* in danger, too, perhaps. But putting her on a bus seemed to offer dangers of its own. How did he know for sure the guy in the T-Bird was interested in *him*? Maybe it was *Daisy* he was pursuing, though that was pretty farfetched. Cripes, he thought, this whole thing was pretty farfetched.

They drove south, passing through Tucson in the late afternoon. It was warm enough so they'd been running the air conditioner in the front compartment for an hour or more, and the desert country and the palm trees increased their impression of heat. The saguaros were in bloom, many of them with white blossoms on the ends of their upraised "arms," and on the distant horizon, looking misty through the smog that hovered over the city, they saw a line of jagged, brown mountain peaks.

Tucson fell quickly behind them, and the desolation wrapped itself around them. What a place to break down, Nick thought uneasily, though the big motor purred as smoothly as ever, and he knew his tires were in good shape.

The blue Thunderbird hung in there behind them, sometimes falling back behind other cars, seemingly content just to keep them in sight. The trouble was, that was too easy. There were a few other recreational vehicles on the road, but it wasn't quite the right time of year for a lot of them. The snowbirds weren't flying back yet from the warm country to their summer homes in the north, school wasn't out so families could take lengthy vacations, and Nick's motorhome stood out like a blood spot on a white sheet. Its sheer size was in distinct contrast to the little mini-motorhomes or campers on the backs of pickups that made up most of the RV traffic. The height that gave Nick such an excellent vantage point for watching the traffic ahead gave a definite advantage to anyone keeping them in view, as well.

Nick couldn't think of anything to do except keep driving.

They didn't talk much. After one or two of Daisy's remarks—such as "If he ran us off the road out there, like down in that arroyo, when nobody else was around, we could lay there for days before anybody found us," and "If he shot us, he could be long gone before anybody would call the cops. We haven't seen a patrol car since we left Phoenix"—Nick finally said, "Shut up, Daisy."

She subsided into silence then, though she didn't seem to be sulking about his brusqueness.

She was undoubtedly right, Nick thought. If they were out of sight of the freeway, amid the scattered yucca and thistle plants, their bones would bleach out like the ones in that famous picture of the cow's skull by that artist who'd lived somewhere out here, New Mexico, he thought it was. What was her name? Georgia O'Keeffe.

Think about something else. Anything else.

If the person driving the dark blue T-Bird had pushed Paul Valerian to his death, why was he now following Nick and Daisy?

He was doing great at thinking about something else, Nick decided wryly.

Suppertime came, but neither of them was hungry. They had replenished their supply of canned pop when they bought gas; there was nothing else they needed. Besides, it wasn't easy to find a place big enough to take a rig the size of this one, and the state-maintained rest stops were few and far between in this country. Mostly what travelers wanted, Nick guessed, was to drive fast and get through to the next site of civilization. In spite of the heat, the desert was chillingly lonely.

Think of something, he told himself angrily. Think of anything except that car behind them, never quite dropping far enough back so that they lost sight of it.

He had little success in thinking of something else. Once, when the T-Bird moved up almost to his back bumper, Nick struck the steering wheel with a fist and exploded in frustration. "What does he want? Does he think I saw him push Valerian, or what? I wasn't even in a *position* to see anything! I had just passed through *under* the overpass! The first thing I *could* have seen was the guy hitting the hood of my car! If he's afraid I could identify him, why hasn't he run me off the road or shot me by this time?"

"Maybe," Daisy ventured, "he wants to intimidate you."

Nick's laugh had a savage note. "Well, he's sure doing a good job of *that.*"

"There's a rest stop coming up," Daisy said as the sign flashed by. "Texas Canyon. Maybe we better eat something, even if we don't feel like it."

"OK," Nick agreed at once, though he knew he was getting paranoid about stopping now. He wished there'd be a state patrol car in Texas Canyon, but it was still a case of "roll up your windows and lock your doors; there's nobody out there to protect you."

There were no cops. Only tourists and traveling salesmen using the rest rooms and eating their evening meals beside the road.

"This is a neat place," Daisy observed as Nick turned off the engine. "It'd be fun to climb some of those rocks." They were magnificent formations, and a couple of little kids whose parents weren't paying enough attention to them were trying to climb a huge boulder set amid strange red "daisies" with yellow-tipped petals and brown centers; Nick had a moment of feeling disoriented, out of time and place, as if he'd suddenly been transported to another planet.

"Don't try it," Nick said about climbing the rocks. "You'd break your neck. Besides, I'll bet this is rattlesnake country." He made no move to get out of his seat.

"I don't want to look. Is our friend still with us?"

Daisy nodded. "Down at the other end. I still can't see what he looks like. Doesn't he ever get out to use the rest room?"

"Well, let's pretend he's not there, and eat. I want to drive as long as I can, and I need extra fuel. How about hot dogs?"

They fixed them together, added some of Elaine Macklin's potato salad, and opened a can of chilled peaches, eating in silence, keeping an eye on the T-Bird in their mirrors. They didn't get out of the coach, not even to let Dillinger run.

"Next time, buddy," Nick apologized as he donated the last half of his fourth hot dog to the pooch. "When there are more people around. OK?"

When they pulled out, they were puzzled to see that this time the blue sedan did not pull out after them, until the answer dawned on Nick. "He *is* going to use the rest room and he didn't want us to get a look at him! He knows he can catch up to us; there's not much of any place we can go to get away from him. The next good-sized place is Las Cruces. I suppose we could try to lose him there, if I can keep driving for that long." He didn't say it with any conviction that it would be possible.

Daisy looked around the interior of the luxurious coach. "Where you going to hide something this big?"

"I don't know," Nick muttered, and then quite abruptly he *did* know. At least it was worth a try. "You hide something in the middle of other things similar to what you want to hide. Get out the book from under the seat, that big fat one that lists all the RV parks and

118

campgrounds. See what's coming up next. We'll stay in one of those."

No way, Nick knew, would he be able to sleep in a rest stop again, especially not if the man following them once more pulled in alongside the motorhome for his own rest. But he'd feel reasonably safe in an RV park, with plenty of other people around.

Daisy consulted the big book, combining it with the information on the map. "There's one in Las Cruces." She read him what the book said about it. "But that's another three and a half or four hours driving, it looks like."

"OK. So we'll go another three and a half or four hours," Nick said at once. "You see any sign of the T-Bird behind us yet?"

"No," Daisy reported a minute later, and they both relaxed a little.

It was Nick who spotted the second car. At first he didn't give it much thought, but after an hour and a half, when they'd made one pit stop and the car pulled in on the opposite end of the parking area, only to follow them out again when they left, an ugly suspicion began to drift into his mind.

Daisy, picking up on his change of mood, turned her head. "What's the matter? I think maybe we lost that guy permanently."

"Maybe so," Nick said, his mouth dry. "But take another look back there. See the second car back?"

Daisy craned her neck to see. "Yeah. What about it? It's bright red."

"A bright red Camaro," Nick agreed. "Just like the one Charlie said he saw by the overpass before Valerian fell. I think we've got us another tail."

11

The red Camaro stayed in their rearview mirrors. They crossed the Continental Divide, passing through high desert country with little to divert their attention, and Nick went over and over in his mind the possible reasons for the surveillance. After a time he couldn't help voicing his thoughts, because the pressure was building to an explosive level.

"It can't be a coincidence," he said as the fading day let the distant mountains lose themselves in the dusk. "A dark blue T-Bird and a red Camaro, just what Charlie said were there at the end of the overpass that night. They *have* to be connected."

Daisy's face was a dim oval in the half-light. "You think that Valerian guy was murdered, don't you? That those men killed him?"

"What else can I think? Yeah, I never believed he'd jumped. I saw his face, just before he died"—Nick swallowed hard—"and I couldn't believe he wanted to die.

I think they threw him over, and the only connection he had with me was that he landed on my car, so what do they want with *me*?"

"If they think you saw something—" Daisy said uncertainly.

"They ought to have figured out I *didn't*," Nick said in a strained tone. "I was under the overpass when they pitched him over, coming out the other side when he hit and smashed my windshield. I'd have told the police if I'd seen anything. The official verdict was suicide, so nobody's looking for a killer. Killers," he amended, thinking of the second car. "And even if they think I somehow saw them, could identify them, why chase me now? If they were going to . . . eliminate me, why didn't they do it while I was still at home? How come they didn't pay any attention to me then, right after it happened?"

"Maybe they did," Daisy said thoughtfully.

"What?" He jerked his head to look at her. "What do you mean?"

"I mean, you and Dill surprised a burglar once, and then that guy climbed in your bedroom window and trashed the place. They're looking for something, Nick. Something to do with what happened to Paul Valerian."

He felt stupid that it hadn't occurred to *him*. Yes, of course. It made more sense than to think that in a neighborhood where the worst thing that ever happened was kids knocking over a garbage can there would be two break-ins in just a couple of days, both to his house. And from the condition of his room, it was clear that they thought there was something there, something they wanted. He remembered how the pockets had been turned inside-out on his jackets, and how the police had concluded the intruder was looking for something small enough to have been carried in one of those pockets.

"I couldn't have anything they want," Nick said, wanting to be convinced. "I don't have anything that belongs to Valerian. I never . . . touched him."

"But they don't know that, for sure," Daisy said, still in that small voice. "And they must think maybe you *do.*"

Nick's laughter was a bit wild. "So where does that leave us? If I had anything, I'd hand it over, only I swear, there couldn't *be* anything! He didn't pass me any messages, hand over any money, papers, nothing! He didn't say anything . . ." He trailed off, trying to make sense of it.

Daisy was taking this more calmly than most people would have, he thought. She wasn't going into hysterics, or losing her head. Or even worrying about her own safety, especially, because she'd inadvertently gotten involved.

"The question is, what do they intend to do? Just keep you in sight and see if you . . . turn up with what they want? Or are they looking for a place to make another 'accident' happen?"

In the face of his own rising concerns, Nick was grateful that she wasn't coming unglued in every direction. "Nice thought, huh? The traffic is dying off, there are hardly any towns out here, nobody much around . . ."

Daisy reached up for the map light, squinting at the fine print on the map spread across her knees. "How far is it to Las Cruces? Maybe we ought to try to stop sooner. What about Deming? It's a small town, but there are people around. And there's a rest stop between Deming and Las Cruces, but it's probably pretty isolated like the rest of the ones we've come to."

"No more rest stops," Nick said decisively. "I think we better try to make it all the way to the RV park just this side of Las Cruces; according to what you read, it's easy to get to, right off the freeway, and it's a pretty good sized one. Even this time of year there'll be plenty of people there, some of them permanent residents. We'll grab enough rest to get us going again and leave early in the morning before there's much traffic on the road. We'll be able to spot anybody following us, for sure."

He didn't say what they'd do about it if the red Camaro was still there. He didn't know.

Again he thought about Steve. Steve was used to dealing with criminals. But Steve was hundreds of miles behind them, now, and he didn't know anybody on any of the New Mexico police departments.

No, Nick thought, he'd go on to Mickey and Uncle Ben. It would have been different if he'd been in a small car; he'd have felt a lot more defenseless. In the motorhome he could see what was coming, and he'd be a lot harder to stop than if he were in a car.

They'd stopped the Pinto by dropping a living human being onto it. But that wouldn't happen again.

It was full dark now. The only things visible were the glowing taillights of the eastbound cars and an occasional set of oncoming headlights.

And the headlights of the Camaro behind him. Nick had memorized the look of them; he could tell when occasionally another car got between them briefly before passing the motorhome. Then the Camaro would come into sight again. Sitting back there, not trying to do anything, but never letting the coach out of sight.

The shock of having a man die in front of his eyes had been bad enough. Nick was beginning to think that this was worse: the insidious fear of the unknown that had been building from the moment he realized they were being followed.

What did those men want? What did they intend to do?

He drove on through the night, which had grown cold once the sun disappeared, so they had to turn on the heat inside the coach. Daisy seemed to have shriveled into her seat, hugging Dillinger who lifted his head to lick her chin from time to time. She didn't talk, and Nick didn't either, but the questions hung in his mind.

Who were they? What did they want? What did they intend to do?

It was too late to register when they pulled into the RV park in Las Cruces. The office was closed, and a sign directed them to choose a site and pay in the morning, so Nick drove on past a row of parked campers and motorhomes and pulled into the first empty space he came to.

When he'd set the self-leveling jacks and killed the engine, the silence around them was almost tangible.

"Jeeze," Daisy said, leaning forward to peer through the windshield. "We're right on the edge of a cliff, and look at the view!"

Las Cruces lay sparkling below them, bigger than

Nightmare

Nick had expected, like a pouch of multicolored jewels spilled onto black velvet, while overhead the velvet was studded with diamondlike stars.

"It's gorgeous," Daisy said, almost in awe. "The stars never look like that at home!"

"You can't see them through the smog," Nick said, but his mind wasn't on the twinkling lights. "Nobody followed us into the park. I deliberately came in at an angle, so I can see the entrance."

"Can a car stay in this place? Or would he have to have a camper or something?"

"I suppose they'd rent him space, if they had it. I've seen people sleeping in station wagons. I'm pretty sure he followed us off the freeway, but he didn't turn in. We should be able to get a decent night's sleep. Then we'll get up and get on the road by about four. Maybe we'll give him the slip," Nick said.

He didn't mention the fact that even if they did, their tracker would probably catch up with them later on. There was only one main road. At Las Cruces, just down the hill, I-25 took off for the north and Albuquerque and Sante Fe. Was there any chance the menacing strangers would think they'd gone that way instead of heading for El Paso?

Nick answered his own question almost at once. No. If they'd been going to Albuquerque, they would have taken I-40 out of California, not I-10.

And the motorhome was so visible. So easy to spot from a mile or so back on the freeway or parked beside the road. Big and white and with those distinctive blue stripes. Oh yes, whoever was following them would find them again when they wanted to.

There was a pay phone beside the office. Nick thought about calling Mickey and telling him what was happening, but his brother and Uncle Ben would be sound asleep by now. They rose early on the ranch, and Uncle Ben wouldn't appreciate having to get up this late to answer the phone. No, he wouldn't call, Nick decided. What could he accomplish except to make Mickey worry about them?

Daisy had soaked in enough of the view and leaned back, looking at him. "Do you think we ought to take turns, keeping watch for those guys? Just in case they decide to sneak up on us during the night? There aren't many lights around, so it wouldn't be hard for them to get close to us without being seen."

Nick considered only briefly. "I don't think they'll try anything here, with all these people around. Most of them have gone to bed, but there must be fifty or sixty rigs in here. There's another one something like ours just up the hill; I noticed it when my headlights swung across it as I turned. Maybe we'll get lucky if that guy is pulling out in the morning, and our red Camaro follows *him*."

They had crackers and cheese and glasses of milk before they got ready for bed. Daisy wiped the white mustache off her upper lip and spoke wistfully.

"I guess there isn't enough water in that tank to let me take a shower, huh?"

"Yeah, sure. We can both take showers." He realized how much he needed one. "Maybe I better hook up the water, though, and use it from the camp. Save what we've got in the tank. I hate to depend on water in strange places. Some of it's pretty lousy. Maybe we can keep enough to last us until we get to Uncle Ben's. The water's good there."

Daisy was smiling. "Great. Can I have the first one? I don't take very long."

"Why not? Hand me my sweatshirt, and I'll walk Dillinger a minute and put him back inside before I hook up."

Daisy had gone after her teddy bear jammies by the time Nick let himself out the door for the second time. It was cold, cold enough so his breath was visible in the night air. Funny country this high desert. By noon tomorrow you could probably fry your brains by going out without a hat.

He'd done the hooking up many times when he was with his dad. He didn't need to plug into electricity, he decided; they would be in a hurry in the morning and wouldn't bother with a cooked breakfast, and the batteries were all up after driving a full day. All they'd need was the water for their showers, so he could save what was in his freshwater tank in case they needed it worse later on.

Nick walked toward the back of the coach, noticing that a few people were still up, watching television or playing music. He heard the faint strains of something classical from the mini in the next parking space.

It was pretty dark between the vehicles. Some RV parks had lights all over the place, but this wasn't one of them. Nick could see enough to tell he wasn't walking into anything, though, and he strode confidently to open the compartment where the water hose was kept.

He leaned over and connected it to the pipes provided between his space and the adjoining one. Then he heard the crunch of gravel under incautious feet. He was half turning to see who it was when the tire iron caught him on the side of the head.

Nick cried out, felt his knees abraded by the gravel, and then his hands. He struggled to retain consciousness, heard a harsh male voice demanding, "Where is it? Hand it over!" and then he succumbed to a deeper darkness, with no stars, no cold, only pain.

12

"**H**ey! What's going on? Whatta you think you're doing?"

The voice came from a distance, but the blackness into which Nick had been plunged was rapidly clearing, though the pain remained.

He'd been hit by something, and hard, and he felt as if his skull had been split. His hands stung, and there was a ringing in his ears.

He felt rough hands on his person, though for the moment he was too disoriented to understand why.

This time the voice seemed nearer, and light streamed out of the mini-motorhome only a few yards away. "Get me the .357, Shirley, somebody's robbing the guy in the next rig!"

The hands suddenly were withdrawn, and there were sounds of running feet, and then there were more hands, but these were gentle.

"You hurt, buddy? Man, he musta really smacked you—with this, looks like. Tire iron. I never hearda anybody gettin' mugged in an RV park, for crying out loud! He get your wallet?"

The couple from the adjoining rig had both come out, the man in work pants and a flannel shirt, the woman in a bathrobe and with her hair in curlers.

Nick took that in before his senses really returned. For a few moments he couldn't make sense of any of it, and then memory began to creep back.

The guy—guys—following them. He put one hand to the spot on his head where a lump had already been raised, and then groped for his wallet. It was half out of his pocket, but still there.

"You're lucky he didn't kill you for it," said the good Samaritan in the flannel shirt. "I'da shot him, by golly, I would. I always carry the old .357 when I'm staying out in the wilds, or in them rest stops, but I never figured I'd have to get it out in a place like this! I'll go call the cops."

By this time Nick's brain was functioning again. "No, no. Don't bother. He didn't get my cash or my credit card, and he's gone now. If the cops come, nobody'll get any sleep tonight, and I'm really bushed. Boy, am I glad you heard something and came out. . . ."

"Nick?" It was Daisy, standing in the open doorway, hugging her pajamas against her chest. Her eyes were wide and scared. "What happened?"

"I'm OK," he said, which was somewhat of an exaggeration. His head felt the way it had the time he and Mickey had been horsing around and he'd accidentally been slammed into the side mirror of his dad's pickup with far more force than his brother had intended. Maybe he felt worse, sort of half-sick to his stomach.

"Thanks a lot, mister. He'd have robbed me for sure if you hadn't come out."

"You sure you don't want me to call the cops?" his rescuer asked. He sounded disappointed.

"No. No, thanks, I'm OK, and he's gone. I just want to get some sleep."

"Well, OK, if you're sure. Good-night, then."

Nick nodded, and then decided that wasn't such a good idea. Daisy moved aside so he could reenter the coach, and he stumbled past her and sank onto the couch. "Better lock the door," he said thickly, dropping his head into his hands while he rested his elbows on his knees.

Daisy flipped the lock switch, then dropped into the chair opposite him. "Was it him? The guy who was following us?"

"I don't know." His voice was muffled. "I never saw anybody, only heard him a few seconds before he hit me. Is my head bleeding?"

Daisy leaned forward to inspect it. Her fingers were very gentle as she parted his hair. "No, but it's got a heck of a big bump on it. A purple bump," she amplified. "Does it hurt something awful?"

"Bad enough," Nick muttered.

"Maybe you ought to see a doctor."

"And get out where the guy can have another crack at me? No, thanks. I'll be OK. Listen, let me take the first shower, all right? If I don't get to bed pretty soon, I'll fall on my face."

"You sure you'll be all right in the shower? What if you pass out?"

"The shower's too small to let me fall down," Nick

told her. He lifted his head slowly, evaluating the pain. "It's getting better. I'm sure I don't have a fractured skull, and I don't think I even have a concussion." He stuck one hand out in front of him. "I only see five fingers. Don't worry."

"If you can't drive," Daisy said, sounding almost hopeful, "I can do it."

He flinched. "Oh, no, you can't. You just barely got past your learner's permit, and you've never driven anything but your Mom's Honda. You're not ready to graduate to a thirty-foot motorcoach."

She was regarding him with concern. "Maybe you ought to call the police, Nick."

His exasperation was in direct proportion to the intensity of his headache. "Daisy, think. Think about how long it takes the cops to work their way through anything. They'd begin by calling Mom and Steve. Waking them up and scaring them half to death. They'd want verification that I had a right to be driving this coach. They'd want to know what I was doing with an under-aged girl—"

"Will you stop referring to me as being underaged? I'll be sixteen in September!"

"Which will still leave you two years shy of eighteen, when you can cross any state lines you want, with anybody. We've crossed two, so far, and will hit another one first thing tomorrow morning. We wouldn't get any sleep for hours, we'd be delayed taking off again tomorrow, and we don't have any time to spare, remember? Not if I'm going to spend any time with Mickey, or you with your sister."

"Are you going to pick me up in San Antonio and take me home with you when you go?"

132

He was too tired to think about it. "I don't know. I hope you're thinking up some way to explain to your folks—and mine—so they don't kill us both."

He thought maybe that was an unfortunate choice of words as soon as he'd said them. Maybe somebody else would kill them—or him, anyway—before his folks knew anything about it.

He got up off the couch, regretting the necessity to move. It didn't do his head any good.

"Didn't the guy who attacked you say anything?" Daisy asked, following his progress through the coach for clean clothes to put on after his shower.

Nick tried to think. "Yeah, he said something about . . . 'Where is it? Hand it over.' He didn't say what. He didn't get my wallet, though, thanks to the guy next door."

"Maybe he wasn't after your wallet."

"Maybe not. But he didn't get anything else, either."

It wasn't until morning that he discovered he was wrong.

Nick woke up when the first gray light of dawn was seeping between the blinds. The coach was cold, and he was chilled through—partly because of the plunging temperature and partly because of the nightmares.

He lay still for a moment, wondering if he ought to get out another blanket or if it was too late for that. He decided it was; they'd better get up and get on the road, but he'd push up the thermostat and give it five minutes to get warm. He found it by touch in the dimness and guessed at how high he was setting it, then crawled back into the bunk.

The last dream lingered in the back of his mind. It was jumbled, confused, but he remembered part of it. A red Camaro, twice as large as the real one, with not only burning headlight-eyes that locked on him wherever he went but gigantic teeth in place of a front grille, ready to devour him.

His head hurt. He ran exploratory fingers over the lump Daisy had described as purple and decided it *felt* purple.

That was certainly not part of the nightmares. The lump on his head was real. The headache was real.

His fear was real.

What was he doing here in New Mexico, where he didn't know a soul? Where the police would surely be suspicious of a seventeen-year-old youth driving an expensive motorhome, transporting a fifteen-year-old girl not related to him, and who had been attacked last night in an RV park?

Cops were naturally suspicious. His mom said Steve didn't mean to be that way toward Nick, it was only that he saw so many kids who were in trouble that he sort of thought of kids that way.

I'm in trouble, Nick thought, listening to the air rushing through the vent, not feeling any of the warmth as yet. So maybe Steve is right about me. I'm no different from the rest of them.

Only Nick hadn't stolen anything. Wasn't guilty of any crime, except maybe stupidity, and he wasn't even sure about that. What else could he have done? At what point should he have done something different?

And the biggest problem of all, what should he do now?

He was as close to Mickey as he was to home. And

he still wanted to see Mickey very badly; in fact, he wanted that worse than ever.

Yet if he was in danger from the man—or men—who followed, he was putting Daisy in danger, too. It was her own fault for doing such a crazy thing as stowing away, but that didn't lessen *his* responsibility.

Would she be safer if he put her on a bus, after all, and sent her either on ahead to her sister's or home to her folks? He had no way of knowing. If it hadn't been for those creeps they'd encountered yesterday, he'd probably have done it. But if there were more creeps on whichever bus they chose, Daisy was vulnerable. She didn't know any more about how to handle those guys than *he* did about dealing with the men who were somehow connected with the death of Paul Valerian.

Somehow connected? Nick's mouth twisted. He couldn't prove it, but he knew what the connection was. They'd murdered Valerian, and now . . . did they intend to murder him, too?

If so, what was taking them so long to do it? No, the guy who'd attacked him last night hadn't been bent on murder, he'd wanted something he thought Nick had. Not money, at least not *just* money. The wallet was right there, in his back pocket, and during those seconds when Nick had been stunned by the blow from the tire iron (Was that a clue? It had never occurred to him to retrieve it as evidence) his assailant could easily have wrested the wallet away from him.

He didn't have anything that belonged to them, that could have belonged to the dead man. But they thought he did. How far were they prepared to go to retrieve something he couldn't possibly hand over to them?

"Nick? You awake?"

He turned his head, and the ache intensified. "Yeah, I'm awake. You get cold?"

"No. Dillinger slept with me. He kept me nice and warm."

"Traitor," Nick said, but without force. "We better get on the road. Maybe we'll be lucky and get through Las Cruces without company."

He didn't really believe that. The driver of the car that had followed them for hours had not followed them at once into the RV park, but he'd left his car outside and come in on foot, armed with the tire iron. He didn't seem the type to let them drive off into the morning sunrise.

"OK. You dress in the bathroom," Daisy proposed, "and I'll dress here."

He was still tired, Nick thought a few minutes later as he studied his own reflection in the bathroom mirror; but if his head didn't hurt, he'd probably feel better by the time he had something in his stomach. He opened the medicine chest and rooted around in its contents until he found a bottle of aspirin, hoping they were still good. They'd been there since before his father died.

For a moment his throat closed convulsively. How long did it take to get over missing someone who had died?

Paul Valerian had died, and no doubt someone was missing him, too. Paul Valerian, who almost certainly had been a murder victim.

He ran water and swallowed the aspirins. When he came out, Daisy was in the kitchen in jeans and with a sweatshirt over her pale green checked blouse. "The toaster doesn't work," she said.

"That's because I didn't hook us up to shore power—to the electricity. And I can't run the generator this time of the morning without waking up all our neighbors. Let's have something cold. When we get a chance to stop, we'll have hot food."

"Cold," Daisy echoed. "Bagels and cream cheese, or cereal?"

They had the bagels, washed down with Pepsi. They ate sitting in the front seats, watching the sky lighten beyond the line of black mountains facing them across the broad valley below.

"They look like castles, or forts, or something. Like somebody carved them into fantastic shapes," Daisy said.

The aspirin was helping a little, maybe. Nick decided he'd live.

At least until the next confrontation with their pursuers, anyway.

He stretched out a leg so he could reach into his pocket for the keys, and then felt the prickle of the small hairs rising on the back of his neck.

"Nick? Something wrong?" Daisy was getting positively intuitive about his state of mind.

Nick gulped, then cleared his throat.

"I think I just figured out what that creep was after last night," he said unsteadily. "He got my keys."

13

Daisy stared at him in consternation. "Your keys? You mean . . . we're stuck here? In New Mexico, with no keys?"

Nick's mouth was dry. "It looks that way."

"But why? I mean, *what's he want?* Just keeping us here won't do him any good! Will it?"

"Darned if I know." It would help if he knew just what they thought they had. "Let me think."

"Is there another set of keys?"

"At home. Dad's set is still hanging on the board in the kitchen. Where mine were until we left." His mind was racing, trying to make sense out of some of this, trying to come up with a solution to their predicament. "Come to think of it, mine and Dad's were the only ones there. Mickey had a set, too. I don't think he'd have taken them to Texas with him. Which might mean they're still here in the coach somewhere."

Daisy ran her tongue slowly over her lips. "Where would they be?"

Nightmare

"Wherever he put them, which could be anywhere. Help me look. In the overhead cabinets, in drawers. Anywhere."

Nick stood up and opened the door over the driver's seat, muttering over his finds. Spare flashlight batteries, shotgun shells, an Oregon map, a pair of his father's sunglasses, a package of gum, a compass on a cord to be worn around the neck. No keys.

He swore softly and moved to the next cabinet. Daisy had moved to the kitchen area and was pulling out drawers, opening cupboards.

"You even carry a hot-air corn popper?" she asked, incredulous, distracted from the search. "What kind of thing is this? Is the printing on it in *French*?"

"Yeah. The only trip Mom and Dad ever took in this thing without us was to Ontario. They bought the popper there. Instructions in both French and English. Come on, brain, think! Where would Mick have left his keys?"

Daisy was still hung up on the popper. "You got any popcorn?"

"Probably. I didn't put any in, but my dad loved it, had it practically every night when we were out somewhere. He usually kept it in that next drawer over."

Daisy opened the drawer. "Yeah, there must be two pounds of it. Jeeze, what a way to travel! My dad will die of envy when I tell him!"

"I'm sure he'll envy the whole trip," Nick said grimly, "especially if you don't get home alive. Look for the keys, will you?"

It was Daisy who found them. "Ta da!" she cried triumphantly, slamming the silverware drawer in which three keys on a plain steel ring had been buried with can openers and steak knives. "These are the right keys, aren't they?"

Nick felt almost limp with relief. "Yeah. Come on, let's get the hell out of here before something else happens."

There was no indication that anyone else in the park was awake when Nick got out to unhook from the water connection. He felt uneasy, but nothing moved, and it wasn't dark enough so anyone could walk up on him again. Daisy stood in the doorway when he turned back; she'd been too nervous to let him out of her sight. She hugged her arms across her chest, shivering. "How come it's so cold? I can't believe it after we needed the air conditioner before!"

"We're up probably four thousand feet," Nick said, not really thinking about either the temperature or the altitude. He was keeping a sharp eye out for any sign of the Camaro or anybody who might be the guy who had hit him last night.

There was still no sign of anyone opening the office, so Nick stuck what he hoped was the right amount of money into the box that housed the electric connections; he was reluctant to walk alone even as far as the office door to put it through the slot that was probably there.

He climbed back into the coach, locked the door behind him—including sliding the dead bolt just in case whoever had his keys decided to let themselves in when he wasn't looking—and slid into his seat.

He turned on the ignition, raised the leveling jacks, and put the transmission into reverse. A dog, tied behind a small trailer, barked once as they passed.

Nightmare

"I have to turn left to get back on the freeway," Nick said as they approached the open gateway. "Look back to the right and see if you spot the Camaro."

There was no traffic. He had time to look himself. No parked cars at all. Yet he was tense, scared, as he eased the big coach onto the road that would take them back to I-10.

For some reason his antagonists had wanted him immobilized here just outside Las Cruces. Why? How angry—perhaps desperate—would they be when stealing his keys didn't work? And why had they chosen that means to slow him down, or keep him in one place? Why risk hitting him over the head and being caught at it, as they had been, when they could have silently moved in and slashed a couple of tires, which would have been just as effective and safer for them?

There were no answers. He swung onto the freeway, eastbound, and still there was no traffic except for an old pickup with half a dozen goats in the back of it. Dillinger barked an enthusiastic greeting at the goats, who paid no attention.

The road took a steep dip down into the valley. The mountains were clearer, now; their shapes suggested an ambitious and massive sculpture. Without the lights, Las Cruces was less lovely, and the country beyond the irrigated fields was dry and brown.

"You ever been across the Rio Grande before?" Nick asked, trying for a semblance of normality as they sped across the bridge at the foot of the hill.

"The Rio Grande?" Daisy echoed, twisting to look back. "That little river is the Rio Grande? I always thought it was a mile wide!"

"So did I," Nick admitted. His stomach was a tight

141

knot as he checked the rearview mirrors. "No sign of anybody behind us yet."

There were a few cars appearing now. People on the way to early jobs, maybe. There weren't enough of them yet, though, to be reassuring. After last night, Nick wouldn't have put anything past the enemy, all the way up to running them off the road and wrecking the coach. Even if it killed them.

And what protection did they have? Even if the freeway was bumper-to-bumper, the way it often was in California, who was going to stop and interfere if the guy in the Camaro decided to run them off the road and then rob them, or whatever he had in mind?

A sign flashed by, giving the distance to El Paso. He didn't look quickly enough to see the mileage, but he knew from the map he'd studied last night that it wasn't more than an hour or so away.

"I'll be glad when we get to Marjorie's," Daisy said.

"Yeah," Nick agreed. The sooner he got rid of Daisy, the better.

It was early enough so they beat the morning rush when they reached El Paso, but there was plenty of traffic. It made them feel better to have other people around, but made it harder to spot a red Camaro behind them, if it was there.

From a trailing car, of course, the motorhome would stand out like a lighted beacon, from far back.

El Paso was an enormous city, spreading out for miles. Across the Rio Grande her sister city of Cuidad Juarez contributed more millions of people to the population of the river valley overshadowed by starkly naked mountains.

Nightmare

Nick concentrated on driving, praying that his assailant of last night thought he'd immobilized the coach and was getting a good night's rest after several long days of driving. *Sleep late, you creep,* he thought. Sleep until I get to San Antonio and turn Daisy over to her sister.

Trucks roared by, heading both east and west. Commuters appeared on their way to jobs in the city. Ranchers came with horse trailers. A few vacationers with little trailers or small motorhomes sped past.

No red Camaro. But Nick couldn't relax, couldn't keep his eyes off the mirrors. The guy was back there, somewhere, and Nick had no doubt that sooner or later he'd turn up again.

They passed a rest stop that had teepees for shelters, and he wished they could stop for a hot meal. It wasn't that he was hungry, but he felt queasy and knew it was at least partly because bagels and Pepsi weren't what he should have eaten for breakfast.

Daisy stirred beside him, shifting Dillinger on her lap. "We ought to eat something pretty soon."

"Yeah. Maybe there's a truck stop somewhere. A long row of trucks might hide the coach."

"You think they're still following us? Even though we haven't seen a sign of them since we pulled out?"

"Don't you?" Nick asked, and Daisy sighed without answering.

The sun was up now so it was hitting them right in the eyes. "It's a good time to stop, until the sun gets a little higher. Yell out if you see anything that looks like a stopping place where we could get out of sight."

Yet there was no such place.

Texas stretched before them, sere and mostly empty. To their right, in the distance, the Rio Grande wound its serpentine way through the valley. There were a few houses close to the city, which they quickly left behind. Sage, mesquite, scattered cactus.

No refuge anywhere, Nick thought dumbly. If he weren't so far from home, if he'd thought Steve would help, he'd have called him. Even if Steve did bawl him out for whatever stupidity had gotten him into this predicament.

But California was far behind, and Steve had no jurisdiction here.

Nick put on his sunglasses and drove on, glad the road was angling to the south now instead of directly east, so the sun wasn't straight in his eyes.

All through Arizona and New Mexico they'd seen signs warning that picking up hitchhikers was not permitted. Other signs indicated the locations of various state penitentiaries. The traveler was left to draw his own conclusions. Hardened criminals were incarcerated in those places, Nick thought. And he had a growing conviction that he was dealing with men like that. Men who would intimidate and even kill to get what they wanted.

Only what was it they wanted? And why did they think *he* had anything to do with it?

Daisy read aloud from another sign. "San Antonio, five hundred and forty miles. We're not going to get there today, are we, Nick?"

"Maybe, if we keep going until late. I'd rather drive than stop." He didn't have to say why.

"There's an inspection station up ahead," Daisy said

suddenly. "We don't have any more fruit, do we? We ate all my oranges."

"It's not for fruit," Nick said after a moment. "It's for wetbacks. Illegal aliens."

They were directed to stop and Nick's heart began to pound. What if he was asked to prove he had a right to drive the coach? What if they asked about Daisy?

He moistened his lips. "Maybe you better go in the back. Lock yourself in the bathroom. No, that might make them even more suspicious. Just stay in the bedroom."

Daisy gave him a startled look. "Why? I didn't just wade across the Rio Grande. I'm an American citizen!"

"Go!" Nick said through his teeth, because he was rolling to a stop and the border patrol in their dark green uniforms were all over out there.

Daisy went. Dillinger hesitated between following her and remaining up front with Nick, finally opting for the girl.

The officer stepped to the driver's side and Nick slid open his window. "Good morning," he said, and then wished he hadn't spoken because his voice sounded funny. They'd think he had a whole motorcoachful of illegal aliens, or escapees from one of the state penitentiaries.

"Good morning. How many in your coach?" the official asked.

"Two." The word almost stuck in Nick's throat. "My sister and me." The lie came out with an effort. What would he do if they demanded identification and saw the difference in their names? Say she's my stepsister, he thought. God, I'm going to be a whale of a liar before this trip is over.

For a moment he thought for sure the man would ask to come inside. Instead, he asked, "Have you made any stops since you came through El Paso?"

"No," Nick said thickly. "We spent the night in Las Cruces, haven't stopped at all."

He held his breath until his chest ached, and then the man nodded. "Don't pick up any hitchhikers," he warned, and stepped backward. He was letting them through!

Nick was wet with sweat when he put the coach in gear and rolled forward. A moment later Daisy asked, "Can I come out now?"

"Yeah. Get me something to drink, will you?"

She brought 7-Up. He'd have preferred a Pepsi, but he didn't ask her to change it.

They gathered speed and blended in with the eighteen wheelers at the maximum allowable speed. If he hadn't been using the cruise control, Nick thought, his foot would have been too heavy to keep them legal; tension made him want to do seventy, eighty, whatever he could get the coach to do. He made himself breathe deeply and try to relax.

"There's an eating place up ahead," Daisy said suddenly. "No truck stop, but there are some trucks there. Could we hide behind some of them, do you think?"

He had to make a pit stop, at least long enough to go to the bathroom, Nick thought. And he'd better fill the gas tank, too. "We'll try it," he said, and flipped on his turn signal.

There were seven or eight big rigs, and after he'd refueled he maneuvered his own coach around behind them to make it invisible from any eastbound traveler.

Nightmare

Now if only the truckers would stay where they were long enough to do some good.

"You want me to fix eggs?" Daisy asked, unbuckling her seat belt when he'd killed the engine.

"Scramble 'em. Or wait, there's frozen waffles. I'll turn on the generator and we can heat those in the toaster; it'll be faster. I don't want to stay here any longer than we have to."

The food sat uneasily on his stomach, but he hoped it would gradually calm him down.

They were climbing again, into the mountains of west Texas. He fought the urge to try to push for higher speeds, knowing it would be disastrous if he did anything stupid that might blow the engine. That would be all he needed, to be stranded and fully at the mercy of a man, or men, who had no mercy.

At least they hadn't had any for Paul Valerian.

Another hundred miles on, Nick actually began to relax a little. They hadn't seen anything out of the way since they'd left New Mexico hours earlier. Maybe they'd finally given the guy the slip, or he'd decided Nick didn't have what he wanted, or there was something else they'd never understand but it meant they were no longer being pursued.

And then Nick glanced routinely into the mirror, and the sweat broke out on his body once more.

At the same moment Daisy said, sounding scared, "The red Camaro's back, Nick."

"Yeah," he agreed, feeling as if his entire body had been shot full of Novocaine. "And that's not all. So's the blue T-Bird."

14

"**N**ick, we've got to tell somebody," Daisy said. Her eyes were huge in her pale face. "Call your dad!"

"My dad's dead. Steve is my stepfather," Nick corrected her almost automatically.

"Well, whatever he is. He's a cop. He'll know what to do."

"He's in California, and he doesn't know any cops here. They won't pay any more attention to a call from him than they would to us, more than likely. Besides, what would he tell the local cops? Two cars we're sure were at the scene of a murder—only, the San Sebastian cops are convinced it was a suicide—have been following us for three days? We didn't have the license numbers of those cars. We can't prove they were there. Charlie Sparks is the one who saw them, not us. And anybody who left California about the same time we did, heading for Texas or points east, would use the same freeway. It's the only one there is this far south."

Nightmare

"But one of them hit you over the head last night and stole your keys!" Daisy protested.

"I can't prove that either. I never saw him. Never saw his car in the park. Unless we want to be taken into protective custody or something like that, the police aren't going to do us any good. And what would that get us, even if they were willing to do it? Nothing. Those guys would just wait around until we walked out and take up where they left off."

"Well, what are we going to do, then?" Daisy demanded. "Just wait until they decide to get rid of us, the same as they did with Paul Valerian?"

Nick drew in a deep breath. "I'm going to call Mickey. See if he can get away from the ranch for a few days. I'm going to ask him to meet me in Galveston."

The scattered freckles were prominent on her nose as she scrunched up her face. "Galveston?" she echoed. "I thought you were going to Houston?"

"Paul Valerian came from Galveston." It was solidifying in his mind even as he spoke. "We don't know anything about him. The police in San Sebastian didn't, either, and didn't bother to find out why anyone would want to kill him. But maybe if we find out who he was, why he was in California, who he knew that might have wanted him dead ... maybe we can figure out some answers. Some way to protect ourselves. Some evidence to take to the police."

Daisy remained doubtful. "Galveston's a long way off yet, isn't it? How far beyond San Antonio?" She rummaged under the seat for the Texas map. "I can't add all those little numbers in my head, but it looks like over a hundred miles more. We can't possibly drive that far tonight—we'll be lucky to make it to San Antonio!"

"I'll stop at the first place I see a telephone and call Mickey," Nick said, as if she hadn't spoken.

"What good's he going to do?" Daisy asked crossly. "He's just another kid, like you. Maybe he's got enough sense to ask your uncle for help, I hope."

There weren't many places to stop, crossing this barren country, at least not ones where there were plenty of people around. Nick didn't dare pause anywhere else.

The altimeter on the dash registered 2,500 feet. The wind was blowing hard, a head wind that would cut down on his gas mileage and slow his speed, Nick thought, trying not to give in to despair.

He almost wished he were driving the old Pinto. It didn't go very fast, and it was hardly comparable in terms of comfort to the motorhome, but it was almost invisible as opposed to this monstrous white elephant.

The red Camaro and the blue Thunderbird hung in there behind them, mile after mile. Sometimes one car was ahead, sometimes the other. Did they think he wasn't aware that they were there? Or was it their intent to intimidate him? And if the latter, what was their purpose? What did they want to frighten him into doing?

If he stopped to use the phone, would anyone try to interfere?

He turned his head to look at Daisy, who looked worried but not panicky. He was grateful for that. He cleared his throat. "Look on the map, will you, and see if you can tell about how far it is to the next rest stop? If there are enough people around, I'll stop and call Mickey."

He should have done it earlier, before they left the

Nightmare

campground, even if it would have meant getting Mickey or Uncle Ben out of bed. This late in the morning he might not be able to reach them; they'd probably be working outside, maybe a mile from the house.

Obediently Daisy studied the map. "They don't seem to have a lot of rest stops in Texas."

"Towns, then. What's coming up in the way of towns? Anything of any size?"

If his pursuers intended to attack him again, he had an uncomfortable conviction that it wouldn't matter whether or not there were other people around. Yet putting himself in a crowd was the only precaution he could think of.

"Towns," Daisy echoed dubiously. "Not many, and they look like crossroads, mostly. Until we get to . . . Fort Stockton."

"How far's that?"

In the mirror the Camaro was falling back, but as he watched the Thunderbird passed it and moved up. Nick ground his teeth.

"A hundred and fifty miles, maybe."

He didn't want to wait that long to call. He was already regretting he hadn't called from Las Cruces. "No rest stops marked between here and there?"

"No. There's a green **X** for a picnic stop. I think that means no rest rooms and no telephones."

Nick swore without apology. "Well, it'll have to be one of the crossroads towns, then. Keep an eye out for a place with lots of cars. They're right behind us, so there's no hope of hiding out in a truck stop."

Twenty minutes later, with the desert having given way to rolling hills turning green and dotted with scrub oaks and cedars, Daisy gave a small cry. "Look! There's a police car, and it's turning in up there at that place . . . it's a gas station and restaurant. Let's stop there. You could even talk to the . . ." A look at Nick's face made her trail off.

"I know how cops are," Nick said. "They're used to kids who goof off, get into trouble, lie, cheat, and steal. And play practical jokes. They're not going to take our word for it that the guys are tailing us and are dangerous. But I'll see if I can get Mickey. We always made a pretty good team, Mickey and me. You want to stay in the coach, or come with me?"

"I'll stay here," Daisy decided after a moment's thought. "I'll watch those two cars, see if anybody gets out that I can get a good look at, and blow the horn if they look like they're coming anywhere near you. Or the motorhome."

"Good," Nick grunted, and once more switched on his flashers for a turn.

The police car was drawing up in the front of the restaurant, the black and white of the Texas Department of Public Safety Highway Patrol arriving simultaneously with another patrol car. Officers got out of each of them, smartly attired in their gray uniforms with red-bordered blue stripes down the sides of the trousers.

Nick breathed a little easier, even as he noticed the Camaro swinging in behind him, keeping its distance. Surely his assailant wouldn't try anything within shouting distance of a pair of armed cops.

"I hope they're staying long enough for me to make my phone call," he said. He wished he could park right beside their cars, but the size of the motorhome made it necessary to pull into a double space out in the middle of the parking area.

He spoke over his shoulder to Daisy as he stepped out. "Lock it behind me just in case they gang up on us."

He heard the click of the lock and the bolt sliding into place as he strode away feeling peculiarly naked as he headed for the pay phones near the front door, which the officers had gone through.

He couldn't resist turning to look back as he entered the booth.

The Camaro had stopped far enough away so that he couldn't see the driver. And when the Thunderbird drew in alongside it, Nick's hackles rose all over the place. There were no doubts in his mind whatever that the two men were the ones who had been seen with Paul Valerian moments before his death, and that one of them had hit *him* over the head last night and swiped his keys. He felt hot and cold all over, at the same time, as he turned his back on them and reached for the phone.

It rang six times and he felt as if his nerves were at the breaking point. "Come on, come on, Mick!" he muttered under his breath. "I *need* you, buddy!"

And then, on the ninth ring, when he was sure nobody was in the ranch house, he heard his brother's voice.

"Hello?"

"Mick! Thank God, I thought nobody was there—"

"Nick? Something wrong?"

"Yeah, you might say that. Listen, I can't explain it on the phone, but I've got some trouble, and I need help. Is there any chance you can meet me in Galveston? I'm

. . . I don't know exactly where I am, to tell you the truth, somewhere east of Fort Stockton. I'm trying for San Antonio tonight, it'll be late, and I'll have to grab a few hours sleep"— Where, he wondered wildly; how?— "and then however long after that it takes to get to Galveston—"

"Sure, I'll meet you. I'm laid up with a bum ankle, that's the only reason I'm in the house, and why it took me so long to get to the phone, but I'll take off in the morning, be there when you get there. We'll have to figure out where to meet."

"I don't know anything about Galveston," Nick said. "Do you?"

"A little. I've been to the beach there. Listen, kid, you in *real* trouble?"

"Yeah, it's real enough. You know we told you about that guy dying when he fell off the overpass onto the Pinto? Well, the official verdict was suicide, but I'm positive that he was murdered. And the guys who did it have been following me ever since I left home."

There was a startled silence, and then Mickey gave a low whistle. "Hey, have you talked to Steve?"

"No. What good's Steve going to do from this distance? I can't prove anything, Mick, that's why I'm going to Galveston. That's where this Valerian guy was from. There must be some clues why they killed him."

"They sound dangerous." He could almost see Mickey thinking furiously. "You in the coach? Kind of conspicuous if you're trying to lose them."

"Tell me about it," Nick said with feeling. "Look, I've got to go. I'm being careful, staying where there are people." He didn't mention having been attacked. "How do we get together in Galveston?"

Nightmare

"Let me think. Cripes, kid, you've sure thrown me a curve. I was cursing because this ankle is going to slow me down—"

"Can you drive?" Nick interrupted anxiously.

"Sure, it's my left ankle. I got me a good set of wheels, automatic. I'll get there. Tell you what. Go straight on through town in Galveston until you get to the street along the water—I can't remember the name of it, but it's impossible to miss—it lies right along the Gulf, beach on one side, big hotels on the other side. Hang a right and go a couple of miles, I think it is; there's an RV park, right on the water, just beyond one of the hotels. Pull in there and I'll either be ahead of you, or I'll get there right after you do. And Nick, take care, OK?"

"OK," Nick agreed. "I'll see you tomorrow afternoon."

He was wringing wet again when he hung up, though the day was not yet hot. The cop cars were still there, only a few yards away. The cars trailing him remained where they'd stopped earlier; nobody had gotten out of either of them.

All his nerve ends were sticking out, but he felt a little better. Mickey knew. Mickey would meet him. There'd never been anything the two of them couldn't handle. At least not up 'til now.

Of course neither of them had been involved in a murder before.

The wind dried his shirt as he walked back across the parking area, leaving him chilled. Daisy unlocked the door when she saw him coming.

"You get him?"

"Yeah. He's going to meet me in Galveston tomorrow afternoon. I was watching those cars. Nobody got out."

"No. But the Camaro has a Texas license plate, and I wrote the number down. I used the binoculars I found when I was hunting for your keys, so I could see that far. I wrote down the number of the Thunderbird, too. Nick, if you called your dad—"

"My stepdad."

"—he could trace them, couldn't he?"

"What good would that do? We need to know more first, and Steve would want to know a *lot* more before he'd try to run down license numbers. And he'd want me to come home, probably."

He slid into his seat, wishing he had the nerve to walk over to those cars and demand to know who the drivers were and what they wanted, but he knew he didn't dare. What if what they wanted was him dead so that he couldn't tell something that he hadn't yet figured out he knew (or they thought he knew) about Valerian's death? What if they simply shot him? No, he didn't dare approach them directly.

The realization made him angry, and he barked at Daisy, who was still looking out the window at the cars. "Come on, buckle up, let's get going!"

Daisy complied without comment, carrying with her a bag of the junk food she'd brought as part of her contribution to the food supply, as well as a couple of cans of pop.

"I wish I could drive, spell you."

"Well, you can't," Nick said, and while he was ashamed of his nasty tone of voice, he didn't apologize.

All he could think of was how far away Galveston, and Mickey, still were.

Nightmare

There were times when their pursuers fell far enough behind that Nick had an irrational hope they'd given up. And then they'd show up in the mirrors again.

He drove at a steady speed, right on the limit. Daisy got up a couple of times to fix something to eat, things Nick could handle without stopping. He only stopped when he absolutely had to, in those widely spaced rest stops amid acres of bluebonnets and some kind of pink and orange flowers he couldn't put a name to, except when they were a variety of scarlet Indian paintbrush. Under other circumstances he might have enjoyed the scenery as they drew nearer to San Antonio.

Daisy was silent for long periods, but once in a while she would stir and draw him out of his dark thoughts. "You ever been to the Alamo?" she asked.

Nick shook his head. "No. I've seen it in movies, though."

"The ones in the movies always make it seem like it was big. Seeing it really, it almost made me cry. I mean, it was so small, and those men who died there trying to defend it from the enemy soldiers, they didn't have a chance. I bet even *I* could get over those walls, they're so low. It's a neat place. If . . . if we get this settled, and you want to stop on the way home, maybe you'd like to see it."

Nick didn't reply. At this point he wasn't sure he was going to survive that long.

Daisy didn't give up. "The River Walk's nice, too. Did you know they were going to cover it over years ago—the river, I mean—and make it into a sewer? Then somebody got the idea of landscaping it, and putting in flowers and walks alongside it—it's down below the level

157

of the rest of the city—and they made it into a tourist attraction. It's really beautiful—"

She broke off, perhaps sensing his rising impatience with her. "Nick, I'll give you my sister's phone number, OK? And you can call me from Galveston after . . . well, when you know anything."

"Sure," Nick said gruffly.

"Be sure to call. I'll get nervous if you don't call," Daisy insisted.

"If I'm alive, I'll call," Nick said.

There was a small silence. Dillinger sat looking between them, wagging his tail helpfully.

"I could go with you to Galveston," Daisy suggested in a small voice. "Maybe I could help, somehow."

Nick was uncompromising. "I'm leaving you at your sister's."

From that point on, Daisy scarcely spoke at all unless it was absolutely necessary.

It was late that night when she directed him through the silent streets of San Antonio to Marjorie's house. She only half remembered the way, and once they took a wrong turn and got into a cul-de-sac that required some strenuous backing and filling before they got out of it.

"This rig doesn't turn on a dime like the Pinto," Nick said furiously. "I don't want to get caught in this kind of place. If those guys showed up, we'd be cut off, and there isn't even anyone awake in any of these houses."

"I'm sorry. I was only here once, and it was over a year ago. I think it must be the next street over." Daisy said in a voice that made Dillinger lick her chin in sympathy.

Nightmare

"I'll be lucky if I find a place to stop this thing," Nick said, so uptight it was a wonder he could think at all. He hadn't seen either of the cars following them since they'd turned into this housing area, but that didn't mean they weren't still there keeping an eye on him. And there sure weren't any people around now.

"Just stop in the street if you have to," Daisy said, subdued. "I'll get my stuff."

That was what he had to do, because the dark street was lined with cars on both sides. He left the motor idling and got out with her to help carry her belongings, marveling at how much she'd managed to stow away without being caught. "When did you tell her you'd get here? She didn't leave a light on for you."

"I didn't know," Daisy evaded, avoiding his eye as she followed him up the walk. "I've got a key to the front door, anyway. I never gave it back to her when I was here the other time."

A car swung into the driveway next door, lights sweeping briefly over them. It made Nick feel as if he'd been spotlighted, that someone would be shooting at them any minute, but nothing happened.

Daisy twisted to allow the dim glow from the street-light to fall into her purse, where she was digging for keys. "They're in here somewhere ... here!"

She was fitting the key into the lock when the neighbors got out of their car and the woman came across the lawn toward them.

"You looking for someone?"

"Oh, Mrs. Garner," Daisy said. "I had to find my key."

"Who is it?" The middle-aged woman squinted, coming closer, then exclaimed in recognition. "Oh,

159

Daisy! I didn't know you were coming. . . ." Her face changed. "Marjorie didn't know, either, did she? No, how could she, or they wouldn't have all gone off for Dallas for that conference of Carl's."

"Dallas?" Daisy echoed faintly, and something seemed to explode in Nick's brain.

"You mean you didn't even tell her you were coming?" He stared down at her, disbelieving. "And now she's not here?"

"Won't be back until at least Thursday, Marjorie said," the neighbor confirmed. "Oh, my. Well, you have a key. Only I don't know if you should be here alone. I'd ask you over to our place until your sister gets back, but the truth is, Harry and I are leaving in the morning. Going to our daughter's up in Waco."

The horn on her car tooted twice, and she turned away, speaking over her shoulder to the pair on the front steps of Marjorie's house. "I've got the house keys, and Harry can't get in without them. I hope you work it out, dear. Good-night!"

Daisy couldn't meet Nick's eyes. "I . . . I called her. Left a message on her answering machine. I never dreamed she wouldn't be here. She's always complaining how she never gets to go anywhere. . . ."

"So you're going to have a nice visit with her empty house," Nick said savagely, wanting to throttle her.

"Nick, I can't stay here. What if one of those guys comes . . . Oh!" She stopped, staring up into his face with an expression that almost brought him out of his fury with her.

"Nick," she said, lifting the ring of keys she carried. "I just . . ." She sounded faint, as if her air had been cut off. "I think . . . I think I just figured out what those guys are after."

And at that moment, a red Camaro nosed around the corner and eased toward them on the deserted street. Its lights were out.

15

D aisy still had the keys in her hand, but the house offered no refuge anyway, Nick thought. Her sister and brother-in-law were gone, and they'd probably be more vulnerable in the house in this quiet San Antonio community than they were in the motorhome.

"Come on," he said, grabbing Daisy's hand. "Run!"

They left her stuff sitting on the steps, except for the purse she had slung over her shoulder.

As they went over the curb, the Camaro's lights came on, bathing them in its beams. Daisy gave the car a frightened look and stumbled on the lower step of the coach, but Nick gave her a shove upward, and bounded in after her.

He didn't wait for her to scramble into her seat, nor to fasten his own seat belt. He was glad he'd left the motor running.

He heard Daisy's rapid breathing and felt her hand grasp the back of his seat to hold herself steady. Nick put the coach into gear and headed directly at the Camaro. In his own headlights it seemed the color of blood.

Nightmare

"Oh, jeeze," Daisy breathed just above his ear, "he's going to block our way out, and there's no place to turn around!"

"The T-Bird's behind us anyway," Nick said. "Hang on, or get down!"

"What are you going to—Oh!"

She went sprawling against the couch behind Nick's seat as he goosed the motor. For a moment he thought they'd hit the Camaro head on; it was deliberately blocking his way on the narrow street, and there were cars on both sides that made it impossible to pass.

Not for nothing had Nick gone four-wheeling with Joe Corelli in the back country. Not that the motorhome was four-wheel drive, but he could do more with it, he thought ferociously, than these suckers thought he could.

Daisy yelped once when the coach hit the curb and went over it, partly in someone's driveway, narrowly missing the car parked to one side. Nick cut sharply to the left almost immediately, heard the scraping of a hedge against the coach sides as he drove through it, and then it was over the curb again. Something crashed and broke in the kitchen area, but he hardly noticed.

This thing wasn't built for high-speed chases, he thought in desperation, or for tight-corner maneuvering. But he was on the street again, past the Camaro.

What the heck did he do now?

Daisy was on her knees in the aisle, then pulling herself onto the couch to look back. "If you turn right at the stop sign," she said, "there's a fire station two blocks over. They don't have guns like the police, but there's someone there all night!"

Nick barely slowed for the stop sign, swinging right.

He didn't have time to glance back, it was too tricky threading his way with this wide rig through the narrow streets, but Daisy moved forward now, flopping into her seat. "They're both coming," she said.

The fire station was not only occupied, there were men out front hosing down a truck. And right beyond the station house was about the best he could have hoped for, with the exception of a police station.

A church with an empty, spacious parking lot.

He took it a bit fast, so that the coach rocked sideways because of the angle of approach and the slant of the entrance across the sidewalk, but that didn't bother him.

It was level now; he'd brought it to a stop, and there were too many firemen under bright lights just a few yards away for their pursuers to do anything foolhardy. At least Nick hoped that was the case. So far they hadn't shown any tendency to shoot from a distance.

Daisy was the first to speak. "I'm shaking all over."

Nick didn't answer. So was he.

Dillinger had climbed onto the couch and was looking out the window; he barked as the Camaro went by.

Daisy's voice was tremulous. "Where's the other one?"

"Don't know. He didn't follow the Camaro. And the Camaro isn't sticking around."

Neither of them felt any better because of that. Beyond the reach of the streetlights, which illuminated only the intersections, the Camaro could stop anywhere, as good as invisible, and keep an eye on them.

"Now what?" Daisy asked.

"Now," Nick said, "we get some rest, I guess. We've

still got to get to Galveston, and I don't know how we're going to do it. The way they boxed us in back there at your sister's I thought they were going to take some real direct action."

"You think they have guns?"

"Well, they didn't *shoot* Valerian. If they wanted to shoot us, I'd think they'd have done it by this time. But I don't think they were cornering us to wish us Happy Birthday or anything like that. We're pretty well lighted here; I don't think they can sneak up on us. If they do anything now, they'll risk being seen from the fire station. It looks as if they're finished washing that truck over there and are going to wash another one. Good. I hope they keep washing trucks out there in front of the station for the rest of the night."

Daisy exhaled in a long sigh. "I've got so much adrenaline in my system it'll be a miracle if I can lie down, let alone sleep."

"Yeah," Nick concurred. "But we'd better try. Do you know how to direct us out of here in the morning?"

"I think so. Back to the left should take us onto one of the main streets and then onto the freeway. Nick."

Her voice changed dramatically when she said his name.

"What? You know, I ought to wring your neck. How could you be so stupid as to come all this way without being sure your sister would even be here? What are your folks going to think if they call and don't get anybody but an answering machine?"

"They'll think we all went somewhere together. They won't worry," Daisy said immediately, but Nick read uncertainty in her eyes.

He sighed. There wasn't much he could do about that at this point, and he was clearly stuck with Daisy for a while longer.

"Listen, Nick." Daisy held up her keys, four of them on a plain steel ring. "Just . . . just before that darned car showed up again, it dawned on me. What the guy wanted who attacked you last night. Keys."

Uncomprehending, Nick made an exasperated sound. "So he *took* the keys! So what?"

Daisy gulped audibly. "So," she said in a small voice, "I think maybe the keys he wanted were *these*."

In the ensuing moments of silence they heard the cheerful voices from the firemen next door, and Nick felt the pounding of his heart. Why did her words fill him with another rush of apprehension, just when he was getting over the last scare?

"Why would those guys want *your* keys?"

Her throat worked again. "Because . . . it just dawned on me, honest, I didn't think of it before . . . "

"What?" Nick rasped, ready to shake her.

"Well, maybe I'm stupid, but I never made the connection until right then when I was trying to find the right key to get into Marjorie's house—"

Nick spoke through his teeth. "Where did you get the keys?"

She inhaled deeply, making an obvious effort to tell it coherently. "The night—the night of the accident, when everybody was milling around, and the police and the ambulance were there . . . I didn't get close to the . . . the body. I never even thought the key ring I found might be *his*, Paul Valerian's. It wasn't anywhere near where he fell."

Nick tried to keep his shifting emotions in check.

"You picked up a key ring . . . with keys on it . . . from somewhere nearby."

"Well, yeah. The light glinted on the metal—you know, from the police cars—and I saw it. It was on the edge of the road, out a ways from the overpass. Back beyond where the police were making people stay. I saw it, and picked it up, and I figured . . . somebody just lost it, you know? It had two keys on it, but no identification. I'd just broke the key ring I had—it was cheap plastic—and I didn't want to spend the money on a new one yet. So I put my keys on it when I got it home— our front door's and Marjorie's—and I watched the lost-and-found ads for a couple of days in the paper, but nobody advertised for it, so I thought it probably wasn't important and I just . . . kept it."

"And left the other guy's keys on it?"

"I tried to get them off," Daisy admitted. "But it's really stiff. I could manage to separate the rings to get my keys on when I wedged the edges between them, but I couldn't pry the inside ends apart, where you'd have to start the keys to get them off. I figured I'd get my dad to do it sometime, but then I never used the keys until I got here, so I forgot about it."

The only light inside the coach came from the globes on tall poles on the street and from the firehouse next door. In the dimness Daisy looked pale and distraught.

"OK, maybe it was stupid, but how did I know? I just thought somebody lost the keys, and they didn't claim them, and it didn't matter. I guess it should have occurred to me when all that guy took from you last night was keys, but I thought he just did it to keep you from moving on."

Nick felt confused and enlightened all at the same time, and even, to his surprise, moderately forgiving. There was a certain amount of logic in what had happened, from Daisy's point of view.

"While I was sitting there on the curb, I saw a little chain somebody had dropped," Nick mused, "made of beer can pull-tabs fastened together. I was in shock, and I picked them up and played with them, the way you do with paper clips when you're nervous. Maybe the guys were watching from a distance, saw me pick something up, and figured I'd found the keys."

Daisy's eyes got wider. "And that's what they were looking for when they broke into your house. The keys!"

It made sense.

It was also scary.

"We could just *give* them the keys," Daisy said tentatively. "Then they'd probably leave us alone, wouldn't they?"

"Maybe," Nick agreed slowly. "And maybe not. They must know we've seen their cars clearly enough to get license numbers. They may not be sure whether or not we could describe either one of them. So they might still think we're a threat to them, that even if they had the keys we could go to the police with information that might lead back to them."

He stared out the window as if to search out their pursuers, but nothing moved on the dark street. "If what we're thinking is true, they murdered a man. They don't deserve to get away with that. And even if we gave them the keys, they might figure they had to shut us up."

Daisy shifted her weight, and something crunched under her foot. She spoke in a dazed way. "Stuff fell out of one of those cupboards when we went over the curb back there. I guess I didn't get the door latched when I was looking for your brother's keys before. This is broken."

"We'll pick it up, before we get cut on it. Close the blinds, and I'll turn on a light."

There was a shattered glass, and silently Daisy swept up the pieces while Nick picked up the other items that had fallen out of the cupboard.

"Let's call the cops," Daisy pleaded as Nick put a deck of cards and several cans of spray paint Mickey had once used to refinish a bike back into the compartment. "We could call from the fire station, right now."

Nick seriously considered that, then shook his head. "They'd keep us tied up for hours—maybe even a day or more, asking questions, running down answers. We still don't have any concrete evidence of what these guys have done, only our own speculations. It's not likely they'd be arrested on what we have, and if we get tangled up with the police, the men are going to be more dangerous than ever, it seems to me. No, I've got to meet Mickey, and then together we'll find out more, maybe. Look, San Antonio must have an airport. Do you know where it is?"

"No," Daisy said at once. "And I haven't got the money for a flight home, anyway."

"Neither have I, but I've got a credit card. Look, the safest thing would be if you took a plane home—"

"And wake my dad up at this time of night to drive into San Francisco or San Jose to pick me up? Give me a break, Nick! He'd kill me!"

"Somebody else may if you stay here," Nick told her soberly.

Her hesitation was brief. "Well, I suppose so, but

I'm more scared to go home than to stay here. If only we could get away from those guys and go on to Galveston by ourselves, maybe we *could* learn something valuable. Be sensible, Nick. I probably couldn't even get a flight out until morning, hours away. What am I supposed to do in the meantime? Sit there in the airport waiting for somebody to sneak up and knock me over the head?"

"It's me they think has their keys."

"OK. But if they think you know that's what they're after, what's to stop them from thinking you gave them to *me*, and sent me away with them?"

Nick was exhausted from a long, tension-filled day of driving and from this latest episode of escaping from men who certainly were dangerous. He hit a hand on the edge of the kitchen sink, grimacing. "If we could only think of a way to get out of here without them seeing us go . . . but there are two of them, and you can bet they've got us under observation right now!"

And then the idea came to him. Simple, though daring, and almost guaranteed to slow down both cars that had been following them.

"What?" Daisy asked, reading his expression. "What did you think of?"

"I think I know how to stop them, if we can pull it off," Nick said slowly. His mind raced, looking for pitfalls. "Kind of spooky, maybe, to do. But . . . I think it would work. Are you game to try something risky?"

Daisy seemed torn between excitement and apprehension. "Maybe," she breathed. "What do we have to do?"

16

Daisy gaped at him when Nick had finished outlining his plan. "You're crazy! We're not going to be able to get away with it! They'll see us coming, maybe shoot us before we even get close to their cars!"

"No, they won't shoot us," Nick said, sounding more confident than he really was. "I mean, if we're dead, we can't tell them where the keys are, and they can't be sure we're carrying them with us. But we're not going to walk up while they're watching us. First we've got to scout out the cars—I'm betting neither one of them is more than a block away—and then we've got to wait until they've had time to think we're staying put for the night. They must have to sleep, too. So we'll rest until we think they've had time to get bored and doze off, and then we'll go do it."

Daisy's tongue snaked nervously over her lips. "Do you really think we can sleep after all of this? And thinking about what we have to do in a few hours?" She was incredulous.

"I'm tired enough to pass out before I even get to my bunk," Nick told her. She didn't know the half of what they'd have to do, but he didn't see any point in telling her the rest of it now. She, too, needed to sleep if she could.

First, though, he had to locate their antagonists. None of the rest of the plan was of any use unless he was sure where the cars were parked.

Daisy balked when he told her he was going out to reconnoiter, alone.

"You can't leave me here by myself!"

"Sure I can," Nick said reasonably. "I'll move faster by myself. But the main thing is, I want anybody watching to think we're still here. So what you're going to do first is take a shower. Light on in bathroom, water running, OK?"

"I haven't got any clean clothes," Daisy said. "They're all sitting on the front steps at Marjorie's."

"Borrow anything you can use of mine. Anyway, after you take a shower, come out and leave the lights on for, oh, five minutes in the front of the couch. Move around a little; anybody watching might be able to see shadows through the blinds, I'm not sure. Anyway, then go back and leave the bedroom lights on for another few minutes, then sit here in the dark. Actually, go to sleep if you can."

Her look made it clear what she thought of that possibility.

"What if you don't come back?"

"That occurred to me," Nick admitted. "But I should be all right. I'm wearing running shoes, I'm going to put on that old camo sweatshirt of my dad's that got left in the closet, and maybe I can find a hat, so I won't look quite the way they've seen me. With any luck I'll be able to walk right past them without attracting their attention. Just a guy on his way home from a late date. But if I don't come back in . . . say, forty-five minutes—"

Daisy emitted a high-pitched squeak. "Forty-five minutes! In that length of time I'll have had two heart attacks!"

"No, you won't." Nick contradicted her with as much authority as he could muster. "And it probably won't take me anywhere near that long. But I'll have to be careful, and there's no way of knowing what'll happen. I don't want you jumping the gun and deciding to panic before it's necessary. You time it, and if I'm gone three-quarters of an hour, unlock the door and walk over to the fire station and ask them to call the local cops."

Daisy drew in a deep breath, steadying herself. "OK. Now, the other thing that's bothering me is, if you think they're watching us right now, how are you going to leave without them knowing it?"

Nick had the answer to that. "I'm going to change clothes, and you're going to do something up front to hold their attention: arrange blinds, look out, change lights, anything. While you're doing that, I'm going out through the back window on the side away from the street. I'm betting they're in their cars, on the street, trying to keep track of us from there. They don't have us in a direct line of vision. There's only one way out of this parking lot, so when we drive out on the street, they'll know it. If we drive past either one of them, they'll know it. But just in case they *can* see us, distract their attention from me when I bail out."

Nick strode toward the back of the coach. "I'm going to change my clothes so I'll look different, and then I'm gone."

It was a relief that though Daisy had a woebegone expression, she didn't argue about the rest of the plan. He hoped she would behave as well when she found out they were going to have to split up for the final, and dangerous, part of the operation.

His words about escaping notice in the simple disguise that was all he could devise had been deceptive. When he went through the window over Daisy's bunk, landing silently on the concrete of the parking lot, Nick's heart was pounding. He stood for a moment, breathing deeply, then cut through the area between the church and an adjoining house to come out onto a side street. That way, if he'd correctly guessed where the Camaro had parked, he'd approach it from the opposite direction than the one they'd expect.

He hoped they weren't expecting anything other than that he'd stay locked in the motorhome.

After what had happened tonight, there was no longer any question that the two cars *were* following the motorhome. And there could be no doubt that Nick's evasive action in front of Marjorie's house had given away his own awareness of the danger his pursuers presented. Both sides now knew they were enemies.

He hoped that they'd underestimate him. A seventeen-year-old kid, even one driving an expensive motorhome, probably wouldn't be perceived as smart enough—or courageous enough—to escape from potential killers. If they figured that way, it might give him a slight advantage.

Nightmare

Nick was sorry he'd had that particular thought. He walked briskly along the darkened street between houses where few lights shown. He'd lost track of time, though he didn't think it could be much past midnight.

The red Camaro was right where he'd expected it to be.

He met it from the front, glad it was dark enough so he could look at it without fear of being recognized. He didn't think either of the drivers of the two cars had really seen him close enough to identify him in the dark, not with the billed cap pulled down to shade his face, and the camo sweatshirt.

If there was anyone in the car, Nick couldn't tell it. He walked quickly past, sure that hostile eyes observed him, sliding a sideways glance toward the Camaro as he passed. There were only black-glass windows, it seemed, with no one visible. Maybe the driver had already fallen asleep, as exhausted as Nick himself, but he doubted it. The sense of being watched was too strong.

For the first hundred yards after he'd passed the Camaro Nick half expected to feel a bullet in the back at any second.

He walked on past the church parking lot, where the motorhome showed a dim glow behind the bedroom blinds, past the fire station where the firemen were now polishing the chief's car, then into the shadows again. The houses were dark except for one where undrawn draperies revealed a late TV watcher.

Again Nick became tense. For his idea to have any chance of succeeding, the Thunderbird had to be no farther away than the beginning of the next block.

It wasn't even that far away. In front of the house

four doors down from the fire station, there it was.

Nick kept going on past it, again trying to determine if there was an occupant. Once more he failed, but as before he was convinced the man was there, probably having slumped down in the seat when he saw Nick approaching.

He hadn't realized he'd been holding his breath until his chest began to hurt, and he let out the air. So far so good.

He returned as he had left the church parking lot, by a circuitous route. No sense in attracting attention by walking past either of the cars more than once.

He tapped once on the window through which he'd escaped, and immediately the blind was raised and the window slid open. Daisy's pale face peered out at him.

"Everything OK?" she demanded.

"They're both even closer than I expected them to be. Listen, I never thought about how I was going to get back in through this window. There're a couple of folding chairs in the bottom of the closet. Hand one of them down to me, will you?"

With the chair as a step stool, he made it back inside, then reached down to retrieve the chair. A moment later he was peeling off the cap and sweatshirt.

"Now," he said with weary satisfaction, "we can sleep for a couple of hours."

He didn't really expect to be able to do it, but almost before he'd gotten comfortable on the bunk, reality began to slide away from him.

The dreams came again, of course. Wild, frightening dreams. Yet he did sleep, though when he roused from a nightmare of being strangled by a faceless figure with incredibly powerful hands he had no feeling of being refreshed.

Nick sat up, and immediately Daisy did, too.

"Is it time to go?"

"I figured about three o'clock. What time you got, can you see?"

Daisy moved across to the side of the couch where a little light could be allowed in by lifting a corner of the blind. "Three-ten. Nick, you really think this has a chance of working?"

He kept his own apprehensions out of his voice. "It's got as good a chance as anything. There's only one thing, Daisy. And don't panic, OK?"

Immediately he felt her tense up. "About what? What did you neglect to tell me? Are we going to get shot?"

"No reason I can think of to believe that. If they were going to shoot us, they'd have done it before now. Put your shoes on, and let's go."

Daisy didn't move. "Somebody broke into your house and shot Dillinger."

"Well, yeah. But like I said, I don't think they want to shoot *us*. They would have by this time. They want to corner us somewhere, maybe, and . . . oh, who knows? Come on."

Daisy still wasn't moving. "What's the one thing?"

"We're going to have to do this simultaneously. The Thunderbird's the closest, so you can do that one. I'll get the Camaro."

She was stunned. Her voice nearly deserted her. "You mean . . . *I have to do it alone?*"

"We probably double our chances if we hit them

at the same time," Nick pointed out as reasonably as he could manage. "If we only put one of them out of commission, that may not be enough."

Daisy said another one of those words he didn't usually hear girls say. "Nick, I can't do it!"

"The heck you can't. You don't want to go back to San Sebastian in a box, do you? That would really be hard to explain to your folks."

"I can't do it," Daisy insisted.

"Put your shoes on," Nick said, and after a moment she bent over to find her shoes and did as he'd ordered.

In the interest of expediency when they came back, Nick had decided to leave the coach unlocked and to carry the keys. Even if their offensive was totally effective, they'd want to get out of there in a hurry.

This time they went out the door on the lighted side of the coach. "If they're not asleep by this time, this probably isn't going to work anyway," he said as he followed Daisy toward the back of the church parking lot. "Remember, now, cut through over there, bear right through the alley so you come out at the other end, then double back along the street."

"What if I don't recognize it?" Daisy demanded in sudden panic. "I'm no great shakes with cars, and it's so dark under those trees! What if I get the wrong car?"

"It'll be the dark sedan in front of the house with the hitching post thing in front of it. There's a light-colored pickup parked right behind it, the only pickup on the block. And remember, the windshield first, then the tire if you get the chance. I'll meet you back here in just a few minutes."

Daisy gave him a scared look, gulped, and took off,

the can of red spray-paint in a hand that was probably as clammy as his own.

Nick didn't bother with the alley or the way around the side of the church. He'd be approaching from the back of the Camaro, and the guy in it would be passed out, he thought positively. It would be quicker going directly to the car. If he was seen by the driver of the T-Bird behind him, he'd be just another guy in jeans and a sweatshirt, coming home late.

It wasn't really cold, and he was bathed in sweat. Nick strode with apparent confidence along the sidewalk, the can of spray paint an awkward bulkiness in his pocket. He hoped Daisy wouldn't fall apart; she was pretty scared.

Well, *he* was scared, too, wasn't he? Anybody with half a brain would be scared. Even if the two mysterious drivers weren't armed, they were menacing enough to make any rational person nervous.

It was a neighborhood much like his own at home; quiet, dark, the kind of place he'd walked at night all his life feeling perfectly safe.

Yet he didn't feel safe.

He approached the red Camaro, which looked almost black under the trees. He cursed the darkly tinted windows, though he probably wouldn't have seen into the car even if there had been no color in the glass. He'd simply have to act as if the man inside were asleep, which Nick sure hoped he was.

Nick had thought about letting the air out of a tire or two, and the idea was tempting now, but he was afraid that might make enough sound to awaken a man who was surely sleeping only lightly. No, better to take care of the windshield first, and then, if that didn't arouse the man from what had to be an exhausted slumber, he might take time to add a flat tire to the damage.

Heart hammering, Nick drew alongside the Camaro and took the pressurized can out of his pocket. He shook it vigorously, and even that minute sound made him apprehensive. Were there eyes beyond the black glass, watching him?

He extended the can over the windshield—get the driver's side first—and depressed the button.

The can hissed gently, spraying black paint over the glass. He couldn't actually see it, but he knew what was happening. Now the other side, and still there was no sign of awareness from the occupant of the car.

For good measure, Nick stepped off the curb to approach the driver's side and on the dying pressure in the can sent the last of the paint onto *that* window.

The car moved as the man inside shifted his weight.

Nick dropped the can into the street and fled; this was no time to pause and let the air out of a tire.

He ran, not quite silently because his feet were hitting the sidewalk hard.

Behind him he heard the car door open, heard a profane exclamation, and Nick poured on the speed.

He looked ahead and saw the lights of the fire station beyond the church, but there were no firemen washing trucks now, and there was no sign of Daisy farther down the street.

What was he going to do if he got back to the motorhome and she wasn't there?

He risked a glance behind him when he came abreast of the church. No running figure, with or without a gun, but the Camaro was easy to spot now. The head-lights reflected off the vehicle parked ahead of it, the taillights blood red in the surrounding darkness.

Nick cut across the parking lot to his own rig, and then he heard running feet coming toward him.

Daisy. They almost collided at the doorway, and he bounded in ahead of her because he was there first, and this was no time to worry about manners. Besides, he was the one who had to start the engine, get the coach moving.

He didn't bother with lights, figuring he could see well enough to stay in the middle of the street. He didn't want to present any more of a target than he already did.

He heard Daisy slam the door and lock it. By the time she stumbled into her seat, he was easing the coach out into the street.

Daisy hadn't belted herself in yet; she was craning her neck to see behind them. "He turned on his lights, but I don't see how he can see to follow us! I got the whole windshield pretty good, I think, before he woke up. I couldn't get a tire—"

"Neither could I," Nick told her, and swung the wheel sharply left as the Camaro, blind though its driver must have been behind a windshield covered in black paint, pulled out in front of him.

There wasn't room to go through between the Ca-maro and a dumpster probably brought in temporarily for spring cleaning and pruning debris. Nick didn't waste time thinking about it. He cleared the dumpster and clipped the Camaro without reducing speed.

Daisy cringed at the resulting racket as the car was

pushed around, deeply dented on its left side. And then they were past it, and on down the street on the route Daisy had said would lead back to the freeway.

Nick hoped his own rig wasn't too badly damaged; Steve would be furious if they wrecked this thing so it couldn't be sold. But there was no time to worry about that now.

He moved through one intersection, then another. There were no lights behind him that he could see.

Daisy's face wore a gleeful grin, somewhat tinged with residual fear, as they pulled onto a cross street with more lights.

"I think we lost 'em," she said.

There was no cross traffic as Nick swung hard left, ignoring the stop sign, and took a deep breath. "I sure hope so," he said fervently.

Daisy reached for her seat belt. "What do we do now?" she asked as Dillinger climbed into her lap and licked her chin.

"Now," Nick told her, "we head for Galveston to see if we can find somebody who knew Paul Valerian. And we hope those guys haven't already figured out where we're heading so they know where to go to stop us."

Already the triumph had begun to fade. "You think they still will? Follow us and stop us from talking to Valerian's family?"

"I'm betting on it," Nick said grimly.

17

An overload of adrenaline kept Nick going for a couple of hours. After that point he would have given a lot for a rest, but he was leery of stopping unless it was possible to do it where the motorhome was completely hidden from the highway, and he didn't come to anyplace like that.

"The paint on their windshields will only slow them down for a little while," he told Daisy as they sped eastward. "And if they think we know what the keys are for, they probably think we know a lot more. Like how to use them, and where. And since the paper published the name of Valerian's hometown, it wouldn't take much to convince them we're heading for it. *They* undoubtedly already know where his family is, and whatever the family knows about his death. So they may be prepared to do anything to prevent *us* from finding it out, if it means they may face a murder rap. Count on it, they're going to be after us as soon as they can get that paint off their windshields. I'm hoping they won't be able to find anything to clean if off right away, but it won't be much of a delay. We've got to get to Galveston first."

Daisy yawned. "It sounds terrible, but I could fall on my face, I'm so tired. It felt like I ran for miles, and I kept expecting a bullet in the back any minute."

Nick managed a grin. "So did I," he admitted. "But maybe they don't have guns. Either that, or they don't want us dead, just . . . " The grin faded. "Just not talking. Or maybe talking only to them."

"But we don't know anything."

"No. But we've got the keys. If worse comes to worst, maybe they'll be satisfied just to take those. Only that way they'll probably get away with murdering Valerian." He glanced at her as she smothered another yawn. "Go in the back and take a nap, why don't you?"

"That sounds good. Only what if you have trouble staying awake? Or what if you need something? I might not hear you if you yelled. If there's . . . an emergency, or something."

"Put your seat back, then, and sleep up here. It reclines, you know. Shift the lever on the left side."

Daisy was asleep at dawn, and for an hour or two after that. Nick was getting hungry, but he didn't find a good place to stop, and he hated to wake her up.

He drove for another hour before his companion stirred, dislodging the little terrier curled in her lap. "Gosh, why didn't you call me?"

"I was thinking about it. There hasn't been any sign of the Camaro or the Thunderbird since we left San Antonio, so maybe we dare to stop long enough to eat and rest a few minutes." There was always the possibility that the men pursuing them had changed cars, that they could be in any of the vehicles behind them, but Nick didn't want to admit that aloud. "Help me pick a good place, OK?"

Daisy leaned forward a few minutes later as they approached an off-ramp leading to several service stations and a restaurant, and Nick gave a grunt of satisfaction.

"A Highway Patrol car and a County Mountie in the restaurant," he observed. "That makes it about as safe as we're going to get. It'll be faster to fix our own food, though."

"What's a County Mountie?" Daisy wanted to know, twisting to see if anyone followed them off the freeway. There was only an ancient rattletrap of a pickup with a young Indian boy driving a load of calves.

"County sheriff's car. I'll drive around to the back parking area just to be on the safe side."

He wasn't sure there was any safe side, but it seemed worth the effort to stay out of sight if he could.

After microwaving French toast and sausages from the freezer, Nick stretched out on the couch. "Let me sleep fifteen minutes," he instructed. "Unless you spot one of those cars before that."

Surprisingly, even a quarter of an hour made a difference in how alert he felt, and he checked the supply of cola drinks. A little caffeine periodically would help, he decided, popping the top on a Pepsi.

As he restarted the engine, he thought of his brother. It was good to know Mickey would be waiting for them in Galveston, that he wouldn't be winging this business by himself anymore.

Nick had decided that rather than stay on the freeway and go through Houston, they would cut across to the south and east on a secondary road. Whether or not the men behind them would figure out they had done this was anybody's guess, and since there were two of them one could take each route to cover all bases, but at any rate he saw nothing in his rearview mirrors that caused him further alarm. Anticipation swept through him when they finally crossed over the bridge into Galveston a little after noon.

"Straight through town until we get to the waterfront, turn right, and go down until we pass the highrise hotels and find the RV park," Nick said aloud.

Daisy was squirming around in her seat. "There are plenty of people around. There's a blue Thunderbird—"

Nick's stomach plummeted in alarm. "—but it's got a woman and two little kids in it. Hey, this looks like an interesting place—"

"Tourist trap, I think," Nick said, negotiating a corner where his big rig took up most of the narrow street.

"Maybe so, but it looks like fun. Wow! There's the Gulf of Mexico! I never saw it before." Daisy looked wistful. "I'd sure like to go swimming in it."

As they topped a slight rise and Nick stopped for a traffic light and signaled for a right turn, she leaned forward again. "Nick, look at the beach! Tourist trap or not, this is a gorgeous place."

"Yeah," Nick agreed, but his mind wasn't on beaches. "There are a few other motorhomes here; we won't be quite as conspicuous, maybe. Keep your eye open for the sign for the RV place."

There was no difficulty in finding the place Mickey

Nightmare

had described, but there was no sign of Mickey. The protective background of probably a hundred other motorhomes and trailers brought Nick a little slackening of pressure, however.

There were dozens of people out under the hot April sun in bathing suits or shorts; most of them were either deeply tanned or sunburned. There were dogs and little kids and old people, and all ages in between; most of them looked relaxed and comfortable, strolling between their rigs and the broad sandy beach.

Nick parked and he and Daisy got out together. They climbed some outside stairs to an office and store on the second floor, which gave them an enticing view of the Gulf and a small lake where two men were water-skiing.

A friendly clerk pushed a registration card toward him, and Nick began to fill it out. As soon as he'd printed his name, the woman said it aloud.

"Corelli? We have a message for Nick Corelli, I think. Just a minute."

Nick froze. Nobody knew he would be here except Mickey, did they?

The woman produced a piece of paper and read from it. "Your brother said he's had car trouble, a fuel pump, he thought, and he'll be here as soon as he can get it replaced." She consulted her watch. "He called about an hour ago."

Nick's mouth was dry. "Did he say where he was?"

"No, I'm sorry, he didn't."

"OK. Thanks," Nick said.

They got instructions for finding their parking space, and Nick guided the motorhome slowly around to a site facing the Gulf. People were crawling over the pale sand like ants, and under other circumstances Nick would have loved joining them.

"Look!" Daisy exclaimed, and then shot him an apologetic glance when he jumped. "I'm sorry, I didn't see *them*, but there's a school of porpoises out there! See, just off to the left?"

"Yeah," Nick said, but he couldn't think about porpoises. "I hope Mickey gets here soon. Until he does, I better try to catch up on my sleep. There's no telling what we'll be getting into from here on."

There was no way anyone could spot his coach from the road, he thought. Not amid all these RVs. There were at least half a dozen rigs the same general size and color of his own. "I'm going to plug into shore power for the air conditioner, and sleep until Mickey shows up." He looked at her then. "Or for an hour. Whichever comes first. In the meantime, if you aren't going to take a nap, why don't you walk Dill in the pet area. Over there where the sign is. And find a pay phone and see if there's a telephone directory."

"Look up Paul Valerian."

"Right."

"What if he's not in there?"

"Well, then we'll have to think of something else," Nick said wearily. The strain and the hours on the road were getting to him.

The hum of the air conditioner drowned out all sounds outside the coach, and he slept deeply, soundly. The nightmares didn't come at once, only as he reluctantly resurfaced out of the soothing depths of sleep.

He sat up then, heart pounding until he realized it

was only the dreams again. How long would it be before he stopped having nightmares?

"Daisy?" he called tentatively, but there was no answer.

He got up and padded in his sock feet into the forward section of the coach. Dillinger raised his head and wagged his tail, and Nick scratched behind his ears.

Daisy wasn't there, but she'd scrawled a note, anchored in the middle of the table with a saltshaker.

"*Paul and Irene Valerian,*" it said, and there was an address in Daisy's scrawling hand.

A little of the tension went out of him. Now if only Mickey would show up.

Nick spun around, startled, when the door opened behind him.

"Oh, hi, you're up!" Daisy said brightly. She sat down on the inside steps to brush the sand off her feet before she put her shoes on. Her fair skin showed a definite pink across her cheeks and the end of her nose. "Boy, would I like to stay here for a while. And really go swimming, not just wading. The water's wonderful." She bent over to tie her shoes, and her voice was muffled. "Of course you have to watch for those stingy jellyfish things; they're all over just above the waterline and they're *huge.*"

She stood up and came the rest of the way into the coach. "I found Valerian's address. He was the only one in the book, so it has to be the right one, doesn't it?"

"Seems like it. I wish Mickey would show up. They gave me a Galveston map at the office. I was just going to look up the address."

"It isn't on there," Daisy said, opening the refrigerator. "I already looked, and didn't find it, so I asked at the office. They told me where it is. I really worked up an appetite. Let's have something to eat while we're waiting for your brother."

But when they'd eaten, Mickey still hadn't come, and Nick was filled with uneasiness. "I think we better go find Valerian's house by ourselves."

"OK. We just keep going east along Seawall Boulevard, out of town. I wrote the directions down. You going to leave a message for Mickey?"

"How?" Nick asked. "We'll have to go in the coach, so I can't leave a note tied to the door handle. Besides that, I don't know if I want a message hanging around if our good buddies show up."

Daisy looked stricken. "I never thought . . . what if they ask about us at the office? They'll find out I asked for Valerian's address!"

"If our coach isn't here, there's no reason they should think the management would know that, or that we'd ever been here," Nick reassured her, hoping he was right about that.

It gave him another idea, though. If their pursuers followed them to Galveston, and they knew this was where their victim had lived, would this put Paul Valerian's family at risk?

"Maybe," Nick suggested with a suddenly dry mouth, "we ought to call Mrs. Valerian. Just in case these creeps show up there before we do."

"Yeah," Daisy agreed at once. "Maybe she'll even know who they are, and what they want."

Five minutes later Nick looked bleak as he hung up the phone. "The number's no longer in service."

Nightmare

Daisy's face was solemn. "So maybe there won't be anybody there, if they've moved away."

Nick considered. "True. Or maybe it was cut off because nobody paid the bill. Anyway, it's the only clue we've got. We'll have to follow through on it. There's nothing else to do."

They found the address Daisy had written down without difficulty. It lay past a series of small houses, down a quarter-mile-long graveled driveway. The house itself was set well apart from its neighbors on a stretch of beach several miles beyond the city limits.

"How come they're all built up off the ground on posts like that?" Daisy asked as Nick eased the motorhome down the long driveway. "Does the tide come in around them, or what?"

"Hurricanes, I'd guess. They blow the water over the land. Why do you think they have a seventeen-foot seawall all along the Gulf side of town? Mickey told me about it; Galveston lost five or six thousand people in a hurricane once, and that's when they built the wall. There's no car here; I hope that doesn't mean nobody's home."

Daisy hugged the little terrier on her lap. "Maybe they only had one car, the one that was in San Sebastian. I mean, this place doesn't look as if the people who live here are rich, exactly. If they don't have two cars, we may be lucky; Mrs. Valerian could be here."

Nick didn't feel lucky. He was about to come face to face with the wife of the man who had died on the hood of his Pinto, and he didn't look foward to it. But maybe Mrs. Valerian knew about the keys.

The drive ended in a graveled turnaround with a

trash barrel in the middle of it. There was no lawn, only the beach grass and the sand. Nick swung the motor-home around the tight circle, so he was headed back the way he'd come.

He killed the engine and for a moment they both sat listening to the cries of the gulls that swooped and soared overhead. The house ahead of them was small and weathered, scoured virtually free of paint by the wind and the salt air; the Gulf of Mexico was so placid now that it was hard to imagine it ever surged this far inland, but the outside stairway to the dwelling on stilts proved that it sometimes did.

Nick had to force himself to get out of the seat and move. "You want to come in with me?"

"Sure," Daisy said at once, though she didn't look any more eager to meet the young widow than he was. "I'll keep an eye out the window, in case anybody else shows up."

"Yeah," Nick agreed around the lump that had suddenly formed in his throat. "Well, let's go."

A curtain fluttered in a window above them as they approached the little house on foot, but there were no sounds, no indication of occupancy. Only a trash fire smoldering in a burning barrel showed that anyone had been around recently.

"What are we going to say to her?" Daisy asked, subdued.

"I don't know yet," Nick said. He started up the stairs, mouth dry and palms wet, with Daisy behind him, and at the top he knocked on the door.

While he waited for someone to respond, he looked over his shoulder to be sure that there was neither a red Camaro nor a dark blue T-Bird coming up the road behind them.

The woman who opened the door looked very young. She wore faded jeans and a red tank top, and she was barefooted.

"Yes?" she asked.

For a moment Nick couldn't get his tongue in gear. "Uh . . . Mrs. Valerian?"

"Yes." Her eyes were dark brown, almost as dark as her hair, and she looked directly into his face.

Behind her, Nick saw signs of packing: In the little kitchen there were cardboard cartons on the floor and the table, and various items both in and out of the boxes.

"I'm sorry . . . it looks like we've interrupted you. . . ." It sounded stupid, but his brain had momentarily failed him.

"I'm packing to move, that's all. Is it something else about . . . my husband?"

Nick swallowed. "Well, yes, it is. Look, could we come in and talk to you for a few minutes? My name's Nick Corelli, and this is Daisy McCallum. We're from San Sebastian, California, and we—"

"Corelli?" To his surprise, the name seemed to mean something to her. She stepped backward, opening the door wide. "Come on in. Excuse the mess, but my dad's coming tomorrow to move us up to my folks' place near Waco."

"Us?" Daisy echoed. She followed Nick inside and positioned herself so that she could see out a window overlooking the motorhome and the driveway beyond it.

"Ronnie and me. My little boy."

Nick flinched. A widow was bad enough. An orphaned child was worse.

Irene Valerian waved a vague hand. "I'm sorry, there's no place to sit down—"

"It doesn't matter. I came—"

"You're the one . . . I remember your name from the newspaper clipping they sent me. Someone was kind enough to think I might want to keep it—" Her throat worked, and her dark eyes filled; however, she blinked away the moisture. "It must have been terrible for you, having someone fall onto your car and die that way."

Under the circumstances, it was disconcerting to encounter concern for himself. Awkwardly, not knowing how to handle this, Nick took out the key ring Daisy had picked up at the scene of the tragedy.

"Mrs. Valerian, do you recognize these keys?"

She took them and separated the keys in the palm of her hand. "This is the house key. I don't know what that one is. Unless . . . " She seemed suddenly breathless. "I think . . . it's a safety-deposit box key."

Nick watched as alarm flooded her face, and his awkwardness fell away. "Would you know how to find out for sure? I mean, do you use a bank here in Galveston? Do you have a safety-deposit box?"

She shook her head. "No. We never had anything valuable enough to put in a safety-deposit box. But—" She was having trouble with her throat and massaged it absently; Nick could see the pulse beating there.

"Do you know of any reason why anyone would try to get these keys away from your husband?"

For a moment she stared blankly. Then her color faded away, and she put a hand on the back of a chair to steady herself.

Nightmare

When she spoke, her lips trembled, as did her voice. "Paul didn't fall accidentally, did he?" she asked. "You're telling me someone murdered him for the key."

It *was* what Nick had been thinking, but it was shocking coming from her.

She swallowed convulsively. "I knew he wouldn't have fallen. Paul was not a . . . a clumsy man." She tried to pull herself together. "Come into the other room where we can sit down. Tell me what you know."

She turned and walked through a doorway. They followed her into a small, inexpensively furnished living room with windows that overlooked the beach and the milky blue-green water.

Nick took the seat she indicated at one end of a couch with a floral slipcover, while Irene Valerian sat at the other end. Daisy remained standing in the doorway, where she could more easily glance out the kitchen windows.

"At this point I'm guessing more than I know," Nick said, his words ragged with emotion. "Do you know why your husband was in San Sebastian?"

"He went there to meet his brother Sal," Mrs. Valerian said readily. "Sal was released from San Quentin just two days before Paul . . . died. Paul didn't want him to come here, didn't want me to meet him. Paul was going to tell him—" She couldn't seem to stop swallowing painfully, and her hands twisted together in her lap. "They *did* kill him, didn't they? Sal and that rotten friend of his, they killed Paul because he told them he wasn't going to go along with them, that he was going to return the money—I told him I wouldn't live with a criminal, and he said he didn't want to *be* a criminal, he wanted to go straight, but he was afraid Sal wouldn't let him—"

There were tears running down her face now, and she wiped them away with the back of one hand.

"Your husband and his brother stole some money," Nick said, wanting to make sense of this as quickly as possible. "And that's what's in a safety-deposit box somewhere? Stolen cash?"

Irene Valerian wept silently as she struggled to maintain her composure. "They robbed a bank out in California, the three of them. Sal and Vitocek and Paul. Paul was driving the car, and none of the witnesses saw him. When they captured the other two, Sal refused to identify Paul, but it wasn't because he was protecting his little brother." She paused to blow her nose on a Kleenex. "It was because Paul had the key to the place where they'd hidden the money. Paul was to leave the money there until the other two got out of prison, and then they'd split it, three ways."

Across the small room Daisy moved restlessly, finally walking back into the kitchen so that she could look out the window over the yard below. Nick unconsciously leaned toward Irene Valerian, aware that he might not have much time. Even if the guys following them had lost track of the motorhome, they might come here, to their victim's widow.

"The other two went to prison, and your husband wasn't ever caught. But he changed his mind about keeping what they'd stolen, is that it?"

"I didn't know any of this when we were married," the young woman said. "I guess I should have been suspicious when I found the bill for the safety-deposit box that came in the mail, but I didn't *want* to be, you know? Paul said it was something of his brother's, and he was taking care of it until Sal got home."

196

Nightmare

This was painful for her, but Nick couldn't let her stop.

"But you found out more? That they'd all been involved in a robbery?"

She made an effort to pull herself together. "I would never have gotten involved with a bank robber. I only found out about it a few weeks ago, when Paul got a letter from Sal from San Quentin Penitentiary. He was getting out and coming home. I wasn't very happy about that. I didn't even learn about Sal until after we were married, and he didn't sound like anyone I'd want to know. Paul acted sort of . . . well, uncomfortable, about the idea of his brother coming here. When he decided to go to California to meet him, to tell him he didn't want to be on the run for the rest of his life and that he wasn't going to hand over the money the way they'd planned, well, I was nervous about it. Afraid Sal and Vito would be very angry, you know. But I was glad Sal wasn't coming back to Texas, that he wouldn't be a bad influence on my husband."

She paused to blow her nose again. "Paul . . . he was a good man, he really was," she said earnestly. "He never got into trouble, except when Sal dragged him into it. After he married me, and we had the baby, he never did anything bad. He was so strange after he got Sal's letter that I finally made him tell me what was the matter, and he promised he wouldn't get involved in any more of Sal's schemes. Paul thought he was already planning another heist of some kind, and he hadn't even been released from prison yet."

"Do you think this Sal is likely to be armed?" Nick asked tersely.

Her laughter held no amusement. "Well, he's been

out of prison long enough to have gotten a gun if he wanted one. He had one when they held up the bank, and so did Vito, I guess. Of course if they were caught with guns, they'd go right back to prison, but maybe he's willing to take a chance on that. Do you know where Sal is?" Her eyes were huge with apprehension.

"Probably not very far behind us," Nick told her honestly, and then filled in quickly with the high points of what had happened. "So," he concluded, "we figure it's the keys he's after. My guess is that he tried to get the keys away from your husband when he found out what Paul intended to do. He wouldn't let him return the money, not after he'd spent several years in prison for taking it. Maybe the keys fell when they were struggling, maybe your husband threw them—they weren't close to the . . . to where he landed—and Sal thought I'd picked them up without realizing I was just fooling with some beer tabs. After he gave up trying to get them back by stealing them, he hit me over the head and got the wrong ones. Then maybe he thought we'd figured out what we had, especially when he headed for Texas. He may believe we're getting together to steal the money ourselves. Do you have any idea where the safety-deposit box is?"

"In California, somewhere. The bank they robbed was in Stockton, and they'd already rented the box beforehand. Sal and Paul each signed for it, so either one of them could get into it, and they'd each had a key— Vito wasn't with them when they signed, Sal didn't trust him that much—but Sal had to ditch his key when he was caught. So there was only the key Paul had to that box."

The way she said it made Nick sit up straighter.

"You mean there was *another* safety-deposit box?"

"Well, I think so. Just a slip Paul made once, that made me think there must be another stash of money somewhere. Maybe in a deposit box, maybe hidden somewhere else. If Paul knew, he didn't tell me. He probably thought it was safer for me not to know. Anyway, he swore he'd never been in on any of Sal's deals before. And in the letter Paul got, about getting out of San Quentin, Sal wrote something about getting a new car to drive to Texas, so I guess there had to be money hidden somewhere."

Nick's thoughts were racing with the implications of all this, and he said slowly, "So whether Sal intended to actually kill him or not, we don't know, but it's a pretty sure bet he was fighting to get the key."

"He'd always led Paul into things," Mrs. Valerian said sadly. "And he probably thought he could go on doing it. Only this time Paul meant it. He had a job, he had me and Ronnie, and he wasn't going to rob banks or have to worry about being arrested any longer. So they killed him."

Nick couldn't think of anything to say to ease her distress. In fact, he was feeling a certain amount of distress himself. Sal Valerian didn't sound like the kind of man who would give up easily, and even if he'd totally lost track of the motorhome, he might think his brother's widow could be coerced into helping him get what he wanted.

Daisy suddenly spoke from the kitchen in a sharp, frightened voice.

"They're coming," she said. "Both of them. The red Camaro and the blue T-Bird. They're right over on the main road."

18

"Is there another way out of here?" Nick asked tersely.

Irene Valerian shook her head. "No. Only a path that goes down to the beach. Just ... throw them the keys. Let them take them away."

"They may not settle for that. After all, we know who they are. And what's in the safety-deposit box. They may want to shut us up, permanently, any way they can. They must have figured out by this time that we've guessed they pushed your husband off that overpass."

"Let's get out of here, lock ourselves in the motorhome," Daisy urged, heading for the door.

"You can't leave me and Ronnie here," Irene said, panic in her face. "Please—Daisy—take the diaper bag there, it's all packed, and I'll bring the baby! Hurry!"

Nick didn't wait for either of them, and there wasn't time to argue. He ran down the outside stairs, leaped into the motorhome and left the door open for Daisy and the Valerians to follow, then started the engine, though the rational part of his mind told him it was probably a lost cause. Dillinger, quivering with delight at his return, jumped into the copilot's seat.

The soil was sandy. A vehicle as heavy as the motorhome would undoubtedly get mired down in it the minute he got it off the gravel. There was only the long, narrow driveway, and the Camaro had already turned into it.

Nick grabbed the CB mike and thumbed the button so that he could speak into it. "Breaker, breaker, channel nineteen," he said, in a voice so hoarse he scarcely recognized it as his own. There was no response, only the slight crackle indicating that the radio was on. "Mayday, Mayday. If anyone hears me, please call the cops. I'm on . . . " His memory failed him; he couldn't even think of the name of the road, let alone the house number.

He heard Daisy and Irene Valerian behind him, but the T-Bird was now coming up the driveway, too, and he didn't look around. Sal and his friend Vitocek—which one was in which car?—were in no hurry. They knew they had him cornered, and this time he couldn't risk going around them in the soft sand.

"Where are we? What's the name of the road?" he demanded, releasing the depressed button so he wouldn't broadcast momentarily.

Irene, carrying a sleepy-eyed little boy perhaps a year old, stood behind him. She, too, glanced toward the approaching vehicles, but she gave him the address steadily enough, and Nick repeated it over the air.

There was no response, only that maddening crackle. Nick swore through gritted teeth. "Our best chance is being overheard by a trucker, but I'm afraid we're too far from Highway 45 for them to hear me. I don't remember seeing a single truck on this road!" Frustrated, not knowing what else to do as the tracking cars crept closer, he switched channels. "Mayday! Mayday! I need help! I'm in a motorhome at"—he paused until Irene again provided the address— "and a couple of thugs who already murdered one man are closing in on me! I've got two women and a baby with me, and I need the cops! If anybody hears me, please call the police!"

He switched to two more channels before he gave up. He had had no indication that his message had been picked up on any of them. There was a possibility that his broadcast had been monitored on a Highway Patrol scanner, but there was no way of ascertaining that. In California, Nick knew, a patrolman could not respond on the radio, but he might answer the call for help in person.

There was no more time to speculate on that.

The enemy had arrived.

"I locked the door, and barred it," Daisy said, sounding breathless. "Can we get around them? Past them?"

It was ironic. There was wide open country in every direction; in a four-wheel drive vehicle Nick could have taken off any way he chose, even along the beach itself. Yet in the motorhome he didn't dare get off the gravel of the driveway or a road.

And as long as the rig was immobilized, a locked door wouldn't hold them off very long. He'd heard Steve on the subject of protecting oneself from intruders and knew that houses were almost impossible to secure totally from anyone determined to get in. And a motorhome wouldn't be any better.

Nightmare

He had swung the coach around when he parked it so that he was headed halfway out of the turnaround. Nick felt cold sweat forming under his arms as the red Camaro rolled to a stop in front of him, and the blue T-Bird barricaded the driveway itself.

There was nowhere to go. Clipping the cars as he went around them, back there in San Antonio, was one thing. Trying to use the coach as a battering ram to run over them or through them was another. All he'd end up doing, Nick realized, was wrecking the coach. He put down the flicker of thought about how much he'd be costing his mother—and Steve—if they couldn't sell it. The thing that really mattered was that it wouldn't help in the end.

Not if Sal Valerian and this Vitocek decided they didn't want anyone left to tell the police about them.

If only he'd made connections with Mickey, he thought.

"That's Sal," Irene Valerian said from where she was standing in the aisle just behind him, jiggling the baby. "I never met him, only saw his picture."

The man had gotten out of the Thunderbird and stood looking at them through the windshield of the coach. Medium height, Nick thought, remembering Charlie Sparks's description. Skinny. Ordinary. Glasses. Nick added, Going bald. And mean looking.

Very mean.

That meant the guy getting out of the Camaro had to be Vitocek. Vito, Irene had called him.

He was ordinary, too. A little taller than Sal, medium build, dark. He had all his hair, and he wore a gold cross on a chain around his neck. A gold cross? Nick was not reassured by it.

Vito looked mean, too.

As far as Nick could tell, though, neither of them was armed. They walked toward the motorhome. Vito stopped in front of it; Sal strolled around to the driver's window.

"Open up," he called.

Nick slid the window open far enough to reply without having to yell. "No, thanks," he said. "Move your cars." He wanted to add, "before I run over them," but it would have been a meaningless threat. Sal knew as well as Nick did that he couldn't push two cars out of the way, even with something as big as the motorhome.

Sal grinned, and the chill that ran through Nick turned the sweat on his body to ice.

This was a man who had recently killed his own brother over possession of a key to a safety-deposit box containing money he'd stolen from a bank. Up to now Nick had considered, at least slightly, the idea that during a struggle Paul Valerian might have fallen accidentally.

Now, suddenly and positively, Nick knew it hadn't been an accident. Paul Valerian had stated his own position on the matter of the crime he had helped commit; Sal had taken steps to see that he didn't manage to follow through.

If Sal Valerian had murdered his brother, he would hardly hesitate to murder his brother's widow and son, and a couple of strangers who meant even less to him. Although maybe, just maybe, he might not want to do it here where there were neighbors around and it wouldn't be taken for an accident. So far the authorities didn't know Sal and Vito had murdered Paul. But if the men killed four people now, including a baby, it was going to be pretty hard to make it look like an accident. And there was a good chance someone in the nearby houses could describe their vehicles.

Nick tried not to seem as scared as he was. "What do you want?"

Sal's widening grin revealed discolored teeth. "You know what I want, buddy. Hand over the key."

For a moment Nick was tempted to do as the man said. Sal was probably going to get it in the end anyway. "Move your car and let me out of here," he said, "and I'll toss it out the window."

Sal laughed. "Try again, kid."

"What happens to us, if I give you the key?"

"Nothing," Sal said, spreading his hands in a gesture of indifference. "All we want is one key. I'm sorry I got the wrong ones, back there in Las Cruces." His pretense of amusement faded, giving him the look of a ferret Nick remembered seeing in a zoo when he was a little kid. "So if you don't want any more trouble, hand it over." His voice dropped, and it was deadly. "I'd hate to have to hurt anybody."

The way he'd hurt Paul, Nick thought, feeling numb, helpless. No matter what I do or say, he intends to kill us.

Yet there was still no sign of a weapon.

Sal addressed his companion without looking at him. "Get a gun, Vito. I'm tired of messing around with this punk kid."

Vito, who had not spoken, turned toward the Camaro. Was it Sal or Vito who had shot Dillinger? Dill suddenly growled, which pretty well answered the question.

"Get down," Nick said over his shoulder to the others.

He sensed movement on Daisy's part as Irene Valerian stared at her brother-in-law with naked hatred on her pale face.

"You killed Paul," she accused. "You murdered your own brother for a few dollars!"

"A few dollars?" Sal echoed incredulously. "I rotted in Q for two and a half years because of those 'few dollars'! I stuck it out because I knew the money was waiting for me when I got out! And then your stupid husband welched on the whole deal! You married a stupid man, lady! He ought to have known me better than that. From the look of this place," he cast a contemptuous glance at the little house on its stilts, "he at least knew enough not to dip into that money for himself."

"He never touched a cent of your dirty money!" Irene said scornfully. "He wasn't a crook like you!"

Behind him, out of his sight, Nick heard Daisy doing something that make a slight sound—opening a window so that she could hear better, maybe?—just before she spoke.

"Somebody's coming."

Nick jerked around, hoping against hope it would be one of the black-and-white Highway Patrol cars, but it was only a nondescript green sedan.

Still, it was a distraction. What could he do with a distraction? What possible option did he have? His mind raced, but it was like a stationary bike; he didn't get anywhere.

"Hurry up, Vito!" Sal barked. "There's a car coming!"

Nightmare

The other houses were too far away, Nick thought in despair. They'd hear gunshots, but by then it would be too late. Voices, even shouting, wouldn't carry to the neighbors. On a day like this, anybody who wasn't at work was probably on the beach, anyway. Out of sight. Unconcerned about a motorhome and a couple of cars at the end of a private driveway.

Vito appeared to have torn out the backseat of the Camaro. He swung around with a sawed-off shotgun in his hands, and Nick felt sick.

"You thought you were funny with that paint on the windshield trick, didn't you?" Sal asked angrily. "Well, there won't be any more tricks, kid. It took us a little time to come up with what we needed, chasing after you that way, but we got it now." He gestured with unmistakable meaning at his partner and the shotgun. "You open up that door, or hand me out the key through the window, and you do it now. Or you're going to get hurt, because we got nothing to lose, see?"

Nothing to lose. The penalty for multiple murders was no worse than that for a single murder. Nick's sickness grew stronger.

And then, as the shotgun was brought to bear on him as he was framed in the open window, Nick's attention was brought back to the green sedan easing up behind the blockade of cars as the driver honked his horn.

Disbelieving, Nick stared.

"Mickey?" he said, and knew a thrill of first hope and then fear, for Vito swiveled to bring the shotgun to bear on the young man who was opening the door.

"Hey, Nick! I'm here!" Mickey called cheerfully. "I'm glad I finally caught up with you. The lady at the

RV park remembered where you got directions to go."

Nick was frozen, unable to think of anything to do except run over the two men who threatened them, and to do that he'd have to start the engine and give them enough warning so they'd get out of the way. And Vito still had the shotgun.

Had Vito had the gun in the car the whole time? Could he have used it when Nick had sprayed paint on his windshield? No, what had Sal said? They had what they needed now, meaning a weapon. They hadn't been able to get the gun until recently, hadn't had it while they were chasing the motorhome across the country, or they'd probably have used it before this.

All his life Nick had heard the expression "made his blood run cold." Now he really understood what it meant. If the gun had been in the car then, they'd have used it.

That meant they'd acquired the gun only after Nick's actions convinced them he knew the significance of the keys, and they'd guessed where he was going, to see Paul Valerian's widow. At that stage, the risk of being caught by the authorities with a weapon, and being immediately reincarcerated, was outweighed by the necessity to get their hands on the rest of the money they'd stashed away.

Figuring out that much didn't help Nick in the slightest to know what to do now.

Mickey strode confidently between the obstructing cars, ignoring Vito and the shotgun, limping a little. "Sorry I'm late, little brother. I only got about twenty miles from home when the fuel pump gave out, and I had trouble finding another one. You have a good trip?"

Nightmare

A scowl was forming on Sal's face, and Vito seemed uncertain about where to aim the gun.

"I hope you're going to come out and give me a proper kind of greeting, after all this time," Mickey said. He was looking directly into Nick's face, and he wasn't stupid. He must have been aware of the danger.

Nothing had changed since his brother's arrival, Nick thought, except that now Mickey, too, was involved in the explosive situation. Yet against all logic, he felt a flicker of hope. "I'll be right out," he said, and slid out of the seat.

Daisy was standing beside the door, one hand steadying herself on the back of the dinette seat. She met his eyes, frightened, yet not panicky.

"When I get out there," Nick said softly, "think up a diversion, if you can. Anything to distract them from us for a few seconds."

Daisy made no reply, and Nick plunged past her down the steps, unlocked the door, and stepped out into the heat of the Texas afternoon. He needed sunglasses, but it was too late to think about that. He felt as if his blood raced at high speed through his whole body, and he only had time to hope that some of it was feeding his brain cells before he walked around the front of the coach and joined Mickey and Paul Valerian's killers.

He saw the pale oval of Daisy's face in the window she had opened a few moments earlier, and then her hand as it came out, throwing something into the burning barrel.

It took him a few seconds to realize what it was she'd thrown.

Shotgun shells. As Nick had improvised with spray

paint, Daisy was trying to create the diversion he'd asked for with shotgun shells.

Only a faint wisp of smoke still rose from the burned trash. Was there enough fire left in the barrel to ignite the shells?

And then there wasn't time to dwell on that, because he'd reached Mickey, who thrust out a hand for a firm, warm clasp.

Had Mickey seen the shells, recognized what they were? Neither of the other men had; Nick was reasonably sure of that. They had turned toward him as soon as he rounded the front of the coach; their backs were to Daisy when she made the pitch.

Nick gripped his brother's hand, releasing it as quickly as he could. He was ready, and so was Mick, when the shells went off.

They exploded almost simultaneously, one of them narrowly missing Sal's head. He ducked, and spun, and so did Vito, swinging the muzzle of the sawed-off shotgun with him, toward the motorhome.

Nick's heart seemed to stop, because Daisy had also let Dillinger out of the coach. The little terrier bounded toward Vito, nipping him on one leg so that the man yelped in anger and pain.

Mickey was closest to Vito and knocked the shotgun down even as Vito pulled the trigger. At such close range, Nick's ears rang, rendering him momentarily deaf, but he didn't need to hear. The blast had missed Dillinger, who was now barking furiously and leaping around Vito's feet, trying for another point of attack.

Nick dove for Sal, knocking him backward, and heard Mickey yell behind him as he drove Vito into the front of the Camaro; Vito screamed profanely, but he'd lost the gun, and the advantage.

Nick had never been much of a fighter, but he'd wrestled around with Mickey and his dad from the time he was a little kid. This time it was for real, and Sal was stronger than he looked. For a moment he was afraid he was losing ground as he struggled with the man, and then Nick threw a shoulder into his opponent and carried him backward as hard as he could, so that Sal's head struck the lower part of the mirror just ahead of the driver's window on the motorhome.

Vito no longer had the weapon, but he hadn't given up. He kicked Dillinger free from one leg and sent him skidding across the gravel, then spun around and moved toward the door of the Camaro. It was still hanging open, and Nick shouted a warning.

"He may have another gun hidden under the back seat, Mick!"

Sal, stunned but coming out of it, suddenly leaped on Nick's back. As they both went down, Dillinger switched his offensive to Sal.

At that point, Daisy yelled from the open window over their heads.

"The cops are coming! They *did* hear you on the CB!"

"Cops!" Vito choked, stopping without plunging back into his car. "Sal, it *is* cops!"

Nick heard the sirens now, and a moment later he saw the cars. Two of them, moving fast, with flashing lights flickering beneath the stilt legs of the houses along the road, coming this way.

Sal gave up trying to pound Nick's face into the

gravel. It wasn't worth it when Dillinger persisted in nipping him about the face and ears. "Let's get out of here," he snarled. "My car, it's faster."

"But all our stuff's in mine," Vito objected.

The patrol cars were turning onto the driveway, and they weren't wasting any time. Nick touched a bleeding lip, winced, and sagged against the side of the coach, catching his breath.

Mickey still held the shotgun, no longer paying any attention to their antagonists as Sal and Vito piled into the Thunderbird and spun wheels, heading off across the sand.

By the time the police arrived, Daisy and Irene Valerian, carrying her little boy, had emerged from the coach to join the boys. Daisy scooped up the still-excited terrier, and Mickey put the gun down against the side of the abandoned Camaro and came to stand beside Nick.

Mickey gave Daisy a lopsided smile. "Nice diversion," he told her.

And then the police were there. One of them stopped; the other slowed, assessed the situation, and decided against pursuing the T-Bird across the sand, instead maneuvering a turn in what was by now a pretty crowded turnaround area. He sped back the way he had come, activating the mike on his radio as he drove.

"Don't let them get away," Irene Valerian pleaded of the officer who was getting out of his car. "They killed my husband, and they intended to kill us, too!"

The officer was six foot four and spoke in a laconic Texas drawl. "Don't worry, ma'am. They won't get far. We've got backup coming from Galveston, and they can't get off the island the other way. There's a deputy sheriff's car on alert about two miles down. Now, somebody want to explain to me what this is all about?"

It didn't take too long to do, considering everything they had to tell, and how many of them there were doing it. The officer was patient, lifting a hand when more than one person attempted to speak at once.

When it was finally over, and Irene had taken the baby inside to change him, the remaining trio stood looking at one another.

"I'm starved," Mickey said, wrapping an arm around Nick's shoulders. "The cop didn't say we had to show up at the police station in the next hour. Let's go into town and get something to eat."

"A big steak," Nick agreed, hoping they couldn't tell by his voice that he was still shaking a little, at least inside.

"A steak?" Mickey echoed. "In Galveston? Seafood, kid, seafood!"

"To tell the truth," Nick admitted with an unsteady laugh, "I'm so empty right about now I'd even appreciate a cup of Mom's cocoa, with marshmallows."

"In case any of this makes the national news," Mickey suggested, "maybe we better call home before they hear about it. There are phones at the RV park we can use, and we better leave the motorhome there. It'll be easier to find a place to park my wheels than yours."

Nick smacked him on the arm with a fist. "It's good to see you again, buddy. Even if you are crazy. Didn't you see that sawed-off shotgun before you got out of your car?"

"Sure, but what else could I do, at that point, except carry it off? I couldn't very well back up and leave you to get shot, if that was what he intended to do. I hoped if I could get you outside with me, we'd think of something, like we always used to do." He grinned at Daisy. "Your girlfriend here did a good job with those shotgun shells. So I played Lone Ranger to the rescue, same as I always did when you got us into trouble."

"You were the one who got us into trouble, not me!" Nick protested, laughing. "And Daisy's . . ."

He'd intended to say she wasn't his girlfriend, which would have been true, but one look at her animated and happy face changed his mind. He'd have to straighten that out, eventually, make her understand that it wasn't that way at all, but Daisy *had* been quick on the uptake, and as gutsy as any guy could have been.

"Daisy did a good job," he conceded, reaching to scratch behind Dillinger's ears. "And so did you, my friend."

Later that evening, with a full belly and his nerves finally almost back to normal, Nick called home. His stepfather answered the phone.

"Hi, Steve. It's me, Nick. I wanted you to know I got here OK, just had supper with Mickey."

"I'm glad you called. Your mom's been starting to worry a little. You know how mothers are. Everything go OK? No problem with the motorhome?"

"No. Well, not exactly. But we did have . . . sort of an adventure," Nick told him. "Uh . . . I hope you won't be mad because we didn't call you earlier, but . . . well, I didn't know how it was going to turn out, see."

Steve's tone sharpened. "You OK, though?"

"Yeah. Fine. Uh, Steve, maybe it'd be better if you didn't tell Mom much about it until I get home. She'll never believe I survived until she sees me."

Nightmare

"You got it," Steve agreed at once. "Speaking of surviving, we've got another neighborhood crisis. That little girl from next door is missing, left a note saying she'd gone to visit her sister in San Antonio, but she doesn't seem to be there. Her folks are in hysterics. You wouldn't happen to know anything about that, would you?"

Nick swallowed hard. "She stowed away in the back of the rig. I didn't know it 'til we were out of California. She's OK."

"I'll tell them. Maybe they'll cool down a little by the time she gets back here, but I wouldn't bet on it," Steve said wryly. "If she was mine, I'd ground her for the rest of her life. So, what's the story? What happened?"

When he'd finished the story, Nick braced himself for an angry response, but it wasn't forthcoming. All Steve said was, "I'm glad it turned out OK." Steve, Nick thought fleetingly, might never take Joe Corelli's place, but he really wasn't a bad guy.

As he hung up the phone and rejoined the other two, Daisy gave him a concerned glance. "Is your dad going to kill you?"

"Not this time," Nick said, and this time he didn't correct her, either.

He was wondering what he might say to her father to keep *him* from killing *her.*

Dorky Daisy had her nerdy moments, but she wasn't really a bad kid, he thought.

"Come on," he said after clearing his throat. "Let's go find the police station and tell them all about Sal and Vito. They must have them in jail by now."

Over Daisy's head, he grinned at Mick, who grinned back.

"OK, but first, let's go back to the coach," Mick said, "and have a cup of cocoa."

It had been a long time since Nick had done much laughing, but it felt good.

Really good.